Trouble in Paradise

**7 sisters.
Plenty of mysteries!**

7 Sister Mysteries

Trouble in Paradise

Ellen Miles

SCHOLASTIC INC.

New York Toronto London Auckland Sydney
Mexico City New Delhi Hong Kong Buenos Aires

ISBN 0-439-36006-4

12 11 10 9 8 7 6 5 4 3 2 1   2 3 4 5 6 7/0

Printed in the U.S.A.   40

First Scholastic printing, April 2002

For Julian and Polly, with love

Trouble in Paradise

Welcome to Paradise!
Cap'n Teddy and "Duchess" Drysdale welcome you and your family
to the most relaxing vacation spot in Vermont:
Paradise Cottages!
Paddle Paradise Lake in a canoe!
Swim from our secluded sandy beach!
Hike the nature trails!
Or just lie back in your own personal hammock
and dream, dream, dream your day away.
10 fully furnished cottages on peaceful
Paradise Lake
Reserve early for the Fourth of July!

Sounds restful, doesn't it? Serene? Halcyon[1], even? You would think so. *I* would think so. And, the truth is, every *other* Fourth of July week my family has spent at Paradise Cottages has been pretty quiet.

But things are not always what they seem. To be

---

[1]halcyon: calm, tranquil. Isn't it a great word? A halcyon was originally a mythical bird that had the ability to calm the wind and waves while it nested on the sea. I collect interesting words, and I'll be sharing some of my favorites with you as we go along. Hope you like them!

accurate, the brochure for this year's visit would look something like this:

Welcome to Paradise!

**Cap'n Teddy and "Duchess" Drysdale welcome
you and your family
to the most nerve-racking vacation spot
in Vermont:
Paradise Cottages!
Get your expensive boat stolen!
See buildings burn to the ground!
Worry that your cottage might be next!
Or run around trying your hardest to
solve the mystery,
putting yourself and your family in danger!
10 flammable cottages on crime-ridden
Paradise Lake
Reserve early for the Fourth of July!**

Chapter One

"Did I tell you what Daniel thinks about my new bike?" Amanda asked.

I nodded. She had. Daniel thought her new bike was "rad." Amanda and I had been together for a total of two hours. We'd picked her up at the bus station on our way out of town, and now we were driving north to Paradise. I already knew what Daniel thought about lots of things. Such as: her bike, her haircut, the color purple, "posers" who can't really "ride" (skateboards, that is), canned ravioli, and sharks.

(In case you're interested in Daniel's opinions, they are as follows, in order: rad, awesome, funky, totally uncool, it *rules*, and awesome.)

Who's Daniel? Amanda's new boyfriend.

Who's Amanda? One of my best friends ever. We grew up together in Cloverdale, Vermont. That's where I still live, along with my parents and four of my six sisters: Helena and Viola, the nine-year-old twins; Juliet, age eleven; and Katherine, who's fourteen. My oldest sisters, Miranda and Olivia, live on their own nearby.

I'm Ophelia Parker, and I'm thirteen. Amanda

Thompson and I hung out so much together when we were little that people said our names as if they were one: OpheliaandAmanda. The Thompsons lived right next door, and Amanda and I spent most of our waking hours together. Also many of our sleeping ones, if you count sleepovers.

Anyway, about a year ago Amanda's parents got a divorce. Amanda and her mom moved to Connecticut, and her dad moved to Boston. The whole thing was incredibly traumatic for Amanda, and I think it still is, judging by the e-mails she sends me. Her parents don't argue quite as much as they used to, but that's only because they don't live together anymore. According to Amanda, they still bicker and squabble every chance they get. And since most of those chances involve Amanda's visits back and forth, she hears the worst of it.

But during the entire two-hour drive up to Paradise Cottages, Amanda hadn't said a word about her parents. All she could talk about was Daniel.

I'd been so psyched about spending a week with Amanda ever since Mom and Poppy agreed that she could come with us to Paradise. We go there every Fourth of July week; it's a Parker family tradition. But this year, Miranda and Olivia both had to work (Miranda's a cop on the Cloverdale force, and Olivia waitresses in Burlington, where she lives and goes to college), so they'd only be visiting for the actual Fourth. Katherine had decided to go to Martha's Vineyard with her friend Amy's family. So I got to invite Amanda!

I *love* going to Paradise, and I couldn't wait to share it all with Amanda: the sparkling, clear blue lake, the fireworks, the cool little winding paths through the woods . . . We were going to have a blast. At least, that's what I'd thought beforehand. Now, I wasn't so sure.

Amanda had changed.

I saw it right away, as soon as we picked her up at the bus. Her lips were pink and shiny, and blond streaks had appeared (as if by magic!) in her reddish-brown hair. The pink tube top she was wearing made it obvious that she'd "matured" a *lot* since I'd last seen her, and her flared jeans were tight and low-slung. She had on pink platform flip-flops that made her look about a foot taller. Suddenly I felt kind of dowdy in my shorts and T-shirt and Tevas.

But it wasn't just the way she dressed, or how she was doing her hair. It was what she talked about, and most of all, the *way* she talked. "He's a total hottie," she gushed, telling me about Daniel. "I mean, the first time I saw him, I was all, 'Wow.' And he was all, 'Wow,' when he saw me. It was, like, love at first sight. Seriously. I am not even joking." She shoved a picture at me. "Is he not a *com-*

plete hottie?" she asked. I caught a glimpse of a shaggy-looking guy in baggy pants before she pulled the picture back and kissed it. Uck. Her lip gloss was probably making it all slimy.

Amanda and I were sitting in the back of our totally overloaded van, which was packed to the roof with all the stuff we'd need for a week. Actually, it was packed *over* the roof, if you count the canoe and the kayak strapped on top. A Beatles CD was blaring (*Revolver*, my favorite), Mom was driving, Poppy was navigating, Helena and Viola were playing Hangman in the first row of seats, and Juliet was sprawled across the second row, reading. She's always been able to read in a moving car, lucky dog. (Speaking of dogs, ours was back home, being taken care of by our pet/house-sitter, Kerry. Bob, our dog, *adores* Kerry, and I think Charles and Jenny, our cats, like her pretty well, too. It's always harder to tell with cats.)

I was hoping that Juliet was really absorbed in her book, because I knew how she would react to the things Amanda was saying. Juliet always speaks her mind, and I was sure to get an earful about my Valley Girl friend. Juliet can't stand girls who talk about "hotties." For that matter, neither can I. But this was different. This was Amanda. My friend Amanda.

I would have liked to tell her about my new

friend TJ, but I knew she'd just make a big deal about him being my boyfriend, and he isn't. Not yet, anyway. But there must be *something* we could talk about, other than boys. We'd always had so much in common. Like — reading! "Hey!" I said, interrupting her latest report on The World According to Daniel. "Did you read the new Rachel Vail book? It's *so* good."

"Like, I am so sure," she said. "Me, have time for reading? As *if*." She stroked her hair back from her face. "Daniel says reading is overrated, anyway. Like, real life is more important, and all."

I sighed and turned to look out the window. It was going to be a long week.

We were deep in the country now. Not that Cloverdale is the big city, but when we drive up north, everything looks different. There are more trees and fewer houses, for one thing. And, as you get closer to Paradise, there are little lakes everywhere. Most of them have lots of "camps" (that's what most Vermonters call their little summerhouses) along the shoreline, and they're full of kids splashing in the water, and people fishing off rowboats. Paradise is a little different. For one thing, it's a big lake, not just a pond. It even has an island right in the middle! And it's very quiet there. You can have a motorboat on Paradise Lake, but there's a speed limit so you can only putt along slowly. You can't go fast enough to pull a water-skier, which is too bad in a way since I'd like to try it, but I guess it's worth it for the peace and quiet.

Speaking of peace and quiet, I was wondering if I was going to have any all week. Amanda just kept on chattering nonstop. In the old days, we would have been singing along with the Beatles, or playing cat's cradle or something. Now it looked as if I was in for seven days of "Daniel says . . ."

"Paradise, three miles!" my mom sang out from the front seat.

"Yay!" I yelled. I sat up straighter to look for all the familiar landmarks: the big old falling-down barn, the house with a chain-saw–sculpted statue of a moose in the front yard, the meadow that's always ablaze with orange and purple flowers. "The creemee stand!" I cried, spotting the soft-ice-cream stand on the edge of town. "Can we stop?"

"We'll go next time we come to town," Poppy promised. "Right now I just want to get all our stuff across the lake."

Oh, I forgot to mention the coolest thing about Paradise Cottages. You can't drive there! Instead, you drive to Paradise Village, which we were just entering, and go straight down to the dock. Then you unload all your stuff into a big motorboat that the Drysdales (the owners) send over. Later, if you need any supplies or if you want to go out for pizza or to the Fourth of July parade, you paddle back over to Paradise in a canoe or get another ride in a motorboat.

It makes it really special, I think. We're all kind of marooned over there on the opposite shore. The people who go to Paradise Cottages every year really get to know one another. I was dying to see Sam Drysdale, the owners' granddaughter and my best summer friend. We've spent the Fourth of July together every year since I can remember.

I looked at Amanda, wondering how she and Sam would get along. If you'd asked me a week ago, I would have said, "No problem." Now, I wasn't so sure.

"Look! Patrick's waiting for us!" Juliet said. She'd put her book away and was climbing out of the van, which Mom had just pulled up to the dock. "He brought the big green boat."

Amanda and I were jumping out, too. "Daniel says green is —" she began. Then she saw Patrick. She never finished her sentence.

Chapter Two

Patrick *was* kind of cute. Even I had to admit it. He'd changed a lot since last summer. I remembered him as gawky and pale and skinny. This year, he'd lost the gawkiness. He was tan and strong-looking, and his hair was bleached blond from the sun.

Patrick is Sam's sixteen-year-old brother. The two of them have always spent summers with their grandparents at Paradise Cottages. I've never even met their parents. Their dad is a journalist and their mom is a biologist, and both of them travel all the time.

Patrick grinned and waved at us. He jumped off the boat and walked over to the van. "Welcome, Mr. and Mrs. P.," he said. He nodded to the rest of us and I saw his eyes pause on Amanda.

"This is my friend Amanda," I said, realizing I should introduce her. "Amanda, this is Patrick."

She giggled. "Hi," she said, shaking back her hair.

"Hi," said Patrick.

There was a brief silence while they stared at each other.

"So," Poppy said finally, rubbing his hands together. "We've got the usual carload of stuff here. Ready to load 'er up?" He nodded toward the boat.

"Aye, aye," said Patrick, giving Poppy a grin and a little salute.

"'Aye, aye' is right," Amanda whispered to me as she watched Patrick follow Poppy around to the back of the van. I had a feeling I wasn't going to be hearing too much more about Daniel for a while.

It took *forever* to unload all our stuff, hauling it out of the van, down the dock, and into the boat. But finally the van was empty. Patrick helped Poppy take the canoe and kayak off the top. "Nice kayak," he said.

"Thanks!" Poppy beamed. "I made it myself from a kit. Did it this winter."

Patrick was impressed, and we had to stand there in the sun while Poppy told him all about the design and how he'd built it. "Think I'll paddle it over myself," Poppy said finally.

"I'll take the canoe," Mom said. "Who wants to come with me? Ophelia and Amanda?"

Amanda turned to me, pleading with her eyes. I knew what she wanted. "No, we'll ride with Patrick," I said.

Helena and Viola climbed into the canoe with Mom.

"Want to ride on the tube?" Patrick asked Juliet. He had a big old inner tube roped to the back of the boat.

"Definitely!" Juliet took off her sneakers, threw them into the boat, and waded out onto the tube while Amanda and I climbed aboard. Then Patrick started the engine, and our little flotilla[2] moved off.

The lake was as sparkly and clear as always. Little waves danced around us, slapping the sides of the boat as we cruised along. I watched the rocky, tree-lined shore recede as Patrick putted straight across the middle of the lake, leaving Poppy and Mom far behind. Puffy white clouds decorated the blue, blue sky, and there was a gentle breeze lifting my hair. I heard the eldritch[3] sound of a loon calling from the far end of the lake, where they always nest. "Ahh!" I said. "Paradise!"

Patrick smiled down at me from his spot in the stern of the boat, near the motor. "Sam can't wait to see you," he said. "She has all kinds of plans for you." He winked at Amanda as he said that. She giggled.

What was *that* about? Sometimes I don't get this boy-girl stuff.

[2]flotilla: a group of ships
[3]eldritch: weird, ghostly, eerie

I decided to ignore it. I trailed a hand in the water as the boat putted along. I turned to wave at Juliet, who was lying happily in the tube. She waved back, a huge smile on her face. I knew she was looking forward to seeing *her* best summer friend, Sally. They were planning to learn to sail Sally's family's Sunfish.

"Look!" I said. "There's Windswept!" That's always the first sign you see of Paradise Cottages. Windswept is one of the Drysdales' cottages. (They all have totally corny names.) It sits a little off from the others on the far side of a little point that juts out into the lake. Just the sight of it made me happy. It meant summer was really starting.

Before I knew it, Patrick was pulling up to the dock.

"Ahoy!"

"Ahoy!" I called back. I waved at Cap'n Teddy. His yachting cap was pushed back over his thick snowy-white hair, and his wide, sunburned face was as friendly as ever as he grabbed the rope Patrick threw him.

"Welcome!" That was Duchess, his wife. She's such a character! I don't know how she does it, but her silver hair is always beauty-parlor fresh, her makeup is perfect, and her clothes look like a magazine ad for "resort wear." She makes the rest of us look like castaways. Her tiny dog, Brinkley, yapped as we climbed out of the boat. She put him down and he ran up and down the dock, barking like mad.

"Ophelia!" That was Sam, running down the path, her long brown braids flying. "I didn't hear the boat coming. You're here! Yay!" We hugged. Then I introduced Amanda to everyone.

"Welcome, Amanda," said Duchess, standing with an arm around Sam. "I'm sure you'll have a marvelous time. Has Ophelia told you about the swimming races? And Regatta Day? And the parade?"

She nodded. I had told her all about it by e-mail. Fourth of July week at Paradise Cottages is crammed full of activities.

Duchess smiled over at Patrick. "Patrick's going to win the race this year, I'm sure of it," she said. "He's on the swim team at school, and he's been training like mad."

Patrick made an "aw shucks" face. Then he grinned and struck a pose, biceps flexed. I heard Amanda gasp.

Nobody else did, though. Because just then, Rinker drove up on the noisy little tractor that is the only vehicle at the Cottages. Rinker is the Drysdales' handyman. I can never quite get a handle on him. He's tall and thin and there's always

14

this stinky little cloud around him because he smokes a pipe, and he never smiles. He works hard, I know that. He's always hammering away at something, or hauling stones to rebuild a wall.

Rinker (I don't even know if that's his first or last name!) climbed off the tractor and hitched up his overalls. He nodded to me and Amanda and Juliet. Then, without saying a word, he started to unload the boat onto the open wagon that was attached to the tractor. He would be making several trips between the dock and Whispering Pines, hauling all our stuff and stacking it on the porch.

I grabbed a backpack and a duffel jammed with snorkels, masks, and fins. Amanda and Juliet picked out their backpacks, too. Then we all started walking along behind Rinker, in a sort of parade. Rinker putted ahead. Cap'n Teddy and Duchess followed him, Duchess carrying Brinkley. Sam and I strolled along next, with Amanda just behind us. And Juliet, whose friend Sally had just dashed down to the dock, brought up the rear. Patrick stayed with the boat, unpacking the rest of our stuff onto the dock.

"Everything looks just the same!" I said happily as we walked up the white gravel path past the common house, where there's a Ping-Pong table and games and books, toward the little white cottages. Each one has a screened porch, furnished with a hammock and an old couch or some easy chairs, and they all look out at the lake.

"It doesn't change much," Sam agreed.

I sniffed the air. There was a smoky smell. "Bonfire last night?" I asked.

She shook her head.

Duchess overheard my question. "No, dear," she said. "Terrible news. The summerhouse burned down."

"No!" I said. The summerhouse was always one of my favorite things about Paradise Cottages. It was a little open-air gazebo covered in flowering vines. Sam and I played in there for hours at a time when we were little. True, in the last few years we didn't go there as much because it was kind of falling apart, but still. I was sad to hear that it was gone.

Duchess nodded sadly. "Yes, it burned to the ground before we could do a thing," she said. "We're not really sure how the fire started." She lowered her voice. "I think perhaps Rinker was a little careless with a match," she whispered to me.

I looked over at Sam and raised my eyebrows. It sounded as if there might be a mystery in the works! Sam and I both *love* mysteries. In fact, one of the games we used to play in the summerhouse was Nancy Drew. We'd always fight about who

16

got to be Nancy and who had to be her "plump friend" Bess.

Sam didn't seem to catch my meaning, or else she ignored it. "Remember how we used to braid the vines?" she asked. "And sometimes we'd pretend we were in a hut on a tropical island, like the Swiss Family Robinson?"

"I remember cutting out paper dolls," I said. "And putting on little plays with them. We made everybody at the Cottages come to see. They must have been so bored!"

She and I reminisced as we walked along. I glanced over at Amanda once in a while to make sure she didn't feel left out, but she was just walking along with this dreamy expression on her face. I had a feeling she wasn't hearing a word we said.

Chapter Three

"Ophelia! Is that you?"

I looked up to see where the voice was coming from and saw the familiar porch of Shangri-La. My family stayed in that cottage once. It has a great view of the island.

"Mrs. M!" I cried.

It was Annette Moscowitz, one of my favorite people at Paradise. She and her husband, Carl, have been coming for years. Last summer, she was very, very pregnant. She could barely walk to the common house. But she loved to swim. "I must be part whale," she'd joke as she bobbed around near the main dock.

"Where's your baby?" I asked.

She grinned. "I have a surprise for you," she said. She turned to call in through the screen door. "Carl!"

Her husband appeared, carrying two squirming girls in pigtails. One had purple ribbons in her black hair and the other had pink, but other than that, they looked exactly alike.

"Oh, my God!" I said. "Twins!"

Annette nodded. "Meet Ava and Rose," she

said. "We knew we were having twins, but we kept it a secret. We couldn't wait for you to meet them!"

"Aren't they adorable?" asked Sam. "Annette says we can baby-sit if we want. I already got to watch them for a few hours the other day."

Amanda just yawned. Which was surprising, because she's always been nuts about babies.

I was dying to hold them and ask a million questions about them, but I was also dying to get to our cottage and check everything out. "I'll come back and visit later!" I told Annette. She and Carl smiled and waved. The twins smiled, too, and made "bye-bye" noises.

"So, who else is here?" I asked Sam.

"Lots of people you know," she answered. "The Wallbridges, of course." That was obvious. Juliet's friend Sally, who was walking behind us, is a Wallbridge. She has a kind-of-cute older brother, Derek, who is always drooping around miserably at Paradise because he can't bring his computer.

"And the Greens," Sam went on. "Tessa's going to give Patrick some competition in that swimming race."

"Who?" Amanda chimed in. Hearing Patrick's name seemed to have woken her up.

"Tessa Green," I told her. "She's the most awesome swimmer. She's a little older than Patrick. I think maybe she's eighteen. She usually wins the swim race in her age group."

"Patrick is sixteen," said Amanda, as if she were telling us something important.

"We know," Sam said, rolling her eyes. "Anyway, Tessa's been swimming a lot every day. You should see how fast she is. Even though she's been a little distracted this summer. She has this boyfriend her parents don't like. She's forbidden to see him. It's a whole big drama, I guess."

"Interesting. Anybody else?" I asked.

Sam thought for a moment. "That's most of the regular people," she said.

"I know Poppy said some regulars couldn't afford to come anymore, since the rates were raised." In fact, Poppy had said this might be the last year *we* could come, but I didn't want to tell Sam that. I thought it was kind of unfair of the Drysdales to raise their rates, but Poppy said they had a right to.

Sam sighed. "It's not *that* much more," she protested. "And anyway, they wouldn't have done it if —"

"Sam, darling," Duchess interrupted. She was walking ahead of us, carrying Brinkley. I didn't realize she'd been listening. "Let's not talk business, shall we? It's too lovely a day for such a dull topic. Anyway, don't you think Ophelia would like to hear about some of our wonderful new guests?" She chucked Brinkley under the chin and kissed his tiny nose, murmuring at him.

Sam shrugged. "Sure, Gram," she said.

"Here are some of them now!" said Cap'n Teddy. "Ahoy there!" He waved at a couple who were sitting on the front steps of Seventh Heaven, along with a little redheaded boy in green overalls.

"Sam, introduce your friend," Duchess prompted.

Obediently, Sam introduced us. "This is Ophelia Parker," she said. "And her friend Amanda. Back there are Juliet and Sally. Juliet is Ophelia's sister. You already know Sally."

"We're the Buxtons," said the woman. She was pretty, with short blond hair and a small, cute face. "I'm Susan and this is Mike." She pointed to her husband, a strong-looking guy with a goatee. "And this is our son, Max."

Max grinned and held up four pudgy fingers. "I'm four!" he shouted.

Just then, Mom and Poppy and the twins caught up with us. They must have left their boats tied up at the main dock. "These are my parents," I said, introducing them. "And my sisters Helena and Viola."

"Helena and Viola!" crowed Max, echoing me. He stared at the twins for a moment. Then he jumped up and ran over to Helena. "Pick me up!" he demanded.

Helena looked a little surprised, but she smiled. How could she not? He was totally adorable. "Well, okay," she said. She put her arms around his waist and lifted him. He giggled loudly, then struggled to be let down. "Now you!" he said, turning to Viola.

"I think Max has some new friends," Mike said. He stood up to shake hands with Poppy.

"Is that Buxton, as in 'Build It Better with Buxton'?" Poppy asked. He was talking about the signs that are all over this part of the state. It seemed like Buxton built almost every new house in the area.

Mike laughed and shook his head. "I wish!" he said. "That's my brother. I'm just a carpenter."

"He's a very, very talented carpenter," said Susan, looking at him proudly.

Meanwhile, Max was telling Helena a "secret," buzzing into her ear. She buzzed back at him and he shrieked with laughter.

"Okay, Max," said Susan. "The Parkers probably want to get settled. You'll see them later. Come on over and sit with us again."

Reluctantly, Max obeyed. But he walked backward, staring at Helena and Viola the whole time. Clearly, they'd made a big impression on him.

We said good-bye to the Buxtons and kept walking. By then, Rinker and the tractor were way ahead of us. He was probably already unpacking the first load of our stuff.

I was going over the cottages in my mind. The Drysdales — Cap'n Teddy, Duchess, Sam, and Patrick — must be in the one called Dunrovin'. They always are. The Wallbridges are always in Dew Drop Inn, and the Greens are in Happy Hideaway. The Buxtons were in Seventh Heaven, the Moscowitzes were in Shangri-La, and we were in Whispering Pines. That left Dunworkin', Bide-A-Wee, Sleepy Hollow, and Windswept.

"Who's in Dunworkin'?" I asked Sam. That's the cottage next to Dunrovin'.

"The Carsons," she told me. She bent to pick up a pinecone, then tossed it into the air and caught it as we walked. "Jack and Rita. They've been here before, but never for the Fourth. They're old friends of my grandparents."

"Old?" roared Cap'n Teddy. "Who're you calling old?" He was laughing, and his face glowed red beneath his white hair.

"I mean," Sam said, pretending exasperation, "they've been friends for a long time."

"Practically forever!" Duchess told me. "Why, I knew Rita when she was a chorus girl."

"And I knew Jack when he was a safecracker!" Cap'n Teddy put in.

"A *safe*cracker?" I asked.

"That was before he retired, of course," Cap'n Teddy said.

"Gramps is joking," Sam said, throwing her arms around Cap'n Teddy and giving him an affectionate hug. "Jack just likes to tell stories. I think he actually sold insurance or something."

Cap'n Teddy shrugged. "If that's what you want to believe . . ." he said, giving me a tiny wink as he hugged Sam back.

I took this all in. The Carsons sounded interesting. I couldn't wait to meet them. Then I went back to my list of cottages. "So, that leaves Bide-A-Wee, Sleepy Hollow, and Windswept."

"Rinker is staying in Sleepy Hollow. Windswept is vacant," Duchess said, a little sadly.

"We're going to do some renovations on those two." Cap'n Teddy pushed back his hat and crossed his arms. "They're a little shabby."

I didn't want to say anything, but so far every cottage we'd passed looked a little shabby. Up close, most of them had paint that was peeling, at least one cracked window, and holes in the screen doors. To change the subject, I asked about the cottage he hadn't mentioned.

"Bide-A-Wee? That's the Wilson fellow," said Cap'n Teddy. "Newspaperman. Says he's here to work on a novel."

"His name's Jeremy Wilson," Sam said, filling in the details. "He's really nice. He covers local politics. But he *really* wants to write mysteries. So he brought his laptop up here for some peace and quiet."

"It's plenty quiet," said Cap'n Teddy. "But I haven't seen him doing any writing. Mostly he just paddles around in that fancy boat of his."

"He has a really nice kayak," Sam explained. "It must have cost thousands."

"Poppy built his own," I told her. "It's purple. He let me choose what color to paint it."

"Cool!" Sam smiled at my dad. "Can I try it sometime?"

"How about" — Poppy checked his watch — "in an hour?" I knew he couldn't wait to show off his boat.

"That might be your best chance," Duchess told Sam. "After all, the next few days are going to be very, very busy around here."

"What's the schedule?" Mom asked.

Duchess ticked off the days on her fingers. "Let's see. Tomorrow's July first. You'll spend most of the day settling in, visiting with the other guests. The big swimming race is on the second, the third is Regatta Day, and of course we'll all go to town for the parade and fireworks on the Fourth."

"And we have to spend a night on the island!" I told Sam. "Like always. And pick blueberries. And make fairy castles in the woods, and hunt for heart-shaped rocks, and do dives off the dock, and —"

Sam grinned and nodded. "We'll do all of it," she said. "And more."

"And more," I agreed, thinking about the mystery of the razed[4] summerhouse.

"I'm ready for a nap," said Amanda, who'd been pretty quiet all along. "And, like, is there a place I'll be able to plug in my blow-dryer?"

I looked at Sam.

She looked at me.

I didn't roll my eyes. But believe me, it took a lot of effort. I had a feeling the whole Paradise experience was going to be wasted on Amanda.

[4]razed: funny word. It sounds the same as raised, but it means kind of the opposite: demolished, torn down.

Chapter Four

"Oh, yay!" I cried. I couldn't help myself. I was so happy to see good old Whispering Pines.

Our little parade had marched right up to it to find Rinker unloading boxes and bags from the tractor. We all pitched in to help, and in a couple of minutes the little trailer was empty, the porch was full, and Rinker had gone off to get another load. Duchess, Cap'n Teddy, and Sam had left, too. "They'll want to settle in, dear," Duchess had said to Sam as they'd gone off arm in arm.

I walked down the porch stairs just to step back and take it all in. Whispering Pines is nestled into a grove of pine trees, so it's all shady and cozy in front. In back there's another porch that gets the early-morning sun. That's the spot to sit in the morning, sipping some tea and looking out at the lake. There's a path that leads straight from the back porch to our own private little dock on the lake, where Poppy's kayak and the canoe would soon be tied up.

There's a hammock on each porch and a bunch of comfy old wooden chairs with overstuffed cushions, perfect for curling up with a good book.

I sighed. "Isn't it the best?" I asked Amanda.

"Don't those cushions get, like, all mildewed?" she asked, wrinkling her nose.

I sighed again, but it was a different kind of sigh. "Actually, I guess they do, a little. They have a certain smell. But I happen to like it." I really do. I guess it's weird, but there's something about that smell that makes me happy. That smell represents summer: long days and warm nights and corn on the cob and ice-cream sandwiches and wet bathing suits and dumb old romance novels to read in the hammock. I love it all.

"Come on in," I told Amanda. "I'll show you around."

She followed me up the porch steps. I pushed open the screen door and took a deep sniff. Ah! That's another smell I love: the scent of the inside of the cottage. It smells of dust and sun-warmed wood and coffee and — I don't know, probably *mice* or something. Okay, so it's not exactly a clean, fresh scent like in the ads for air freshener. But it's one of my favorite smells in the whole world.

I looked around at all the old familiar sights. There were the old couches in the big, open living room, all squashed and soft and cozy and covered in brightly colored but faded Indian-print bedspreads. The fishing nets up on the wall. The tacky sign that says, WELCOME, FRIENDS!

"Where's the TV?" asked Amanda.

"No TV," I told her. "No TV, no phone, no fax, no computer."

"No phone?" She looked a little panicky.

"There's one at the common house," I reassured her. "If you need to check in with your parents or something. And if somebody calls you, they'll come and get you." I knew she wasn't totally happy about that, but what could I do? "Come see the kitchen," I said. I pulled her into a large room to the right. "Isn't that the coolest?" I asked, pointing to the old-fashioned black cookstove.

"You mean, we have to chop wood in order to cook?" Amanda was looking even more panicky now. "Is there running water?"

I laughed. "Yes, there's water," I said. "And *two* bathrooms, one with a shower and everything. Plus a shower outside, for when you're all sandy from the beach. And no, we don't have to chop wood. See? There's a regular stove, too." I glanced around at the kitchen, loving the sight of all the old plates and bowls lined up on the open shelves. The dishes are white enamel with a red rim and a picture of a rooster on them. In the middle of the kitchen is a big old white-painted table, covered with a red-and-white-checked tablecloth. There was a vase of white daisies on the table. Sam had probably picked them and put them there for us.

"Are you hungry?" I asked Amanda, trying to

remember to be a good hostess. I kind of hoped she wasn't, since all the food was still packed in boxes and bags out on the porch.

She shook her head. "Where do we sleep?" she asked. "Do we have, like, a bedroom?"

For a second I felt like saying, "No, we sleep in hammocks out under the trees," just to see her face. But that was mean. "We have the *best* bedroom," I said. "Come see!" I led her out of the kitchen. The living room is two stories high in the middle, but all around it at the second level is a balcony. "The bedrooms are up there," I said, pointing. I headed for the staircase near the back of the cottage, the one that goes up to the right side. There are two bedrooms over there. On the other side, there are two bedrooms and a tiny bathroom.

Amanda and I had the front corner bedroom, the one I usually share with Juliet. Juliet would be in the other one, where Katherine usually sleeps. The twins would sleep in one of the bedrooms on the other side, and Mom and Poppy would be in the other.

I threw open the door to our bedroom. It looked the same as always. There were the two twin beds, covered in the old familiar bedspreads, one blue and one red, both with pictures of horses and lariat-tossing cowboys on them. White curtains billowed at the windows as a pine-scented breeze blew in. There was another little vase of flowers on the big old dresser, which had a lacy white cloth covering at least some of its chipped blue paint.

I drew in a breath. "The shark picture!" I said, pointing to a painting over the dresser. It showed a man clinging to the wreckage of a ship, watching with a frightened face as the fin of a shark drew ever closer. I *love* that picture. I don't know why. I guess it's just part of the whole Paradise thing for me.

"Ew," was Amanda's only comment.

"There aren't any sharks in the lake," I assured her.

She rolled her eyes at me. "Like, I'm not *stupid*," she said.

Just then, my mom called from downstairs, "Ophelia! Amanda! Can you girls come help us unpack?"

I slipped between the sheets later on that night, feeling completely content. We'd unpacked all our stuff, and Poppy had made an excellent dinner. Afterward, Amanda and I had strolled down to the common house for ice-cream sandwiches. Sam had met us there and walked us back, and we'd hung out on the back porch until we were too tired to talk anymore.

I pulled the cowboy blanket up and snuggled down into my bed. Ah, Paradise.

Chapter Five

It was raining when I woke up. Not hard, just a steady soft rain I could hear on the roof. I didn't mind. It often does that on summer mornings in Paradise. I knew it would clear up soon.

I rolled over to check my watch, which I'd left on the night table. It was only ten after six! No way was Amanda going to want to get up that early. But I couldn't sleep anymore. I slipped out of bed, grabbed some clothes, and padded out onto the balcony to pull them on. Then I tiptoed downstairs, grabbed Juliet's purple rain jacket off one of the hooks near the door, and let myself out.

I walked down the main path, loving the quiet, gentle rain and the way it made everything smell and look so fresh and green. The common house was shut up and quiet, so I went right past it and down to the main dock, where Poppy's kayak and our canoe were tied up, along with a bunch of other boats. I walked to the end of the dock and gazed out at the fog that was just starting to lift off the lake. The water's surface was like a mirror.

Everything was so still. It was preternaturally[5] quiet. I heard a loon call and smiled to myself.

Then I heard a splashing noise. And it kept coming nearer.

For a second, I remembered the scary stories Katherine used to tell me about a lake monster. There was a whole summer when I wouldn't go *near* the water because of those stories. Finally, Poppy found out what I was scared of and set me straight. Katherine got in big trouble: She didn't get any ice cream for a whole week.

The splashing sound was even closer now. Finally, a figure emerged from the fog. It was a swimmer! The person was moving along like a regular motor, with strong, even strokes.

I watched until I could see who it was. "Tessa!" I said as she drew up to the dock.

She looked up, her eyes wide. "Whoa! You scared me! I didn't think anybody would be out this early." Then she pulled herself up onto the dock and shook her head to get the water out of her ears. She was tall and thin and really strong-looking in her blue racing suit. She glanced around. "Training swim," she explained, even though I hadn't asked. "Anybody else up?"

[5]preternatural: beyond the ordinary

"Just me," I said.

She looked relieved, like she didn't want to see anyone else. "How are you, Ophelia?" she asked.

"Great," I said.

She smiled. "Me, too. But I have to go in. I'm freezing!" She didn't have a towel or anything.

"Bye," I said, watching her run off toward Happy Hideaway.

I sat on the dock for a while longer, until the rain let up and the sun started to break through. Then I decided to walk some more. I headed for one of the little winding paths that go through the woods. But before I got there, I smelled that smoky smell. The summerhouse! How could I have forgotten? I had to go check that out.

I walked past the common house again, up a little hill, through a grove of birch trees, past the big, moss-covered boulders Sam and I call Momma and Poppa Bear, and into a little clearing. My stomach lurched when I saw the blackened, charred timbers that were all that was left of the summerhouse.

I tiptoed around, looking for clues. It was probably too late to find much; detectives always say you have to get to a crime scene when it's still fresh. It looked as if a lot of people had trampled through the area; there were way too many different types of footprints for them to be any kind of clue. There were even tire tracks, probably from Rinker's tractor, and marks from someone trying to rake the cinders into a neater pile.

I poked a toe into a pile of logs, moving the top one a little so I could see what was underneath.

Nothing. Just more blackened logs. Poor old summerhouse.

Then a glint of red off to the side caught my eye. I bent down to see what it was and picked up a red metal screw top, about two inches in diameter. Probably just the top off some juice bottle or something. But I put it in my pocket, anyway.

While I was bent over, I saw something else interesting. A small pile of paper matches, bent at weird angles. I felt a little chill run down my spine. This must be the exact spot where somebody started the fire! It hadn't been easy, apparently. There were at least ten matches piled up there.

I looked around some more, but didn't see anything else suspicious. Then I started thinking again about all the things that Sam and I used to do in that summerhouse, and I got so sad I had to leave.

Something about being at Paradise makes me kind of sentimental, I guess.

Anyway, I walked back down toward the common house. Just as I passed it, Sam walked out of

Dunrovin'. "Hey!" I called. "Come for a walk! Better grab your raincoat."

"Don't have one," she said lightly. "Where should we go?"

I was just thinking about the possibilities for our oblectation[6] (the waterfall? the wild apple orchard? the secret cove?) when I heard a commotion down at the dock.

"What's going on down there?" I asked.

Sam shrugged. "Don't know. Somebody banged on our door a little while ago, but I was still half-asleep. Gramps went out, that's all I know."

"Let's go see," I said. We ran down to the dock. A bunch of people were standing around: Cap'n Teddy, Mike Buxton, Derek Wallbridge, and two men I didn't know, one grandfatherly looking and one younger.

"Who're they?" I whispered to Sam. She knew who I meant.

"The old guy is Jack Carson," she whispered back. "The one in the baseball cap is Jeremy Wilson. The reporter?"

I nodded. "He looks mad," I said. Jeremy Wilson seemed to be yelling at Cap'n Teddy.

"He sure does," Sam agreed. She started walking faster, then broke into a run.

[6]oblectation: delight, pleasure

I followed her. Soon we were close enough to hear.

"I'm *not* losing my temper," Jeremy Wilson was saying. "But I might soon. I don't know if you realize how much that boat is worth! If it's been stolen, *your* insurance is going to have to cover it."

"Oh, my God!" Sam said, covering her mouth with her hand as she stared at the dock. "Jeremy's kayak is gone!"

Chapter Six

First a fire. Now a missing boat. Something was rotten at Paradise Cottages! In all the years I've been coming here, there had never been a crime wave like this one.

Sure, the summer when I was six my stuffed dachshund, Doogie, turned up missing one morning. A toy-napping? Not exactly. In the end I discovered that Mom had taken him over to Paradise Village along with the laundry. A fresh, clean Doogie and I were reunited that very afternoon.

Another time, somebody was helping themselves to ice-cream sandwiches from the freezer in the common house and not leaving money for them (the snack bar is run on the honor system). But that turned out to be Derek Wallbridge, who had spent all his savings on a new computer game and had to wait for his next allowance so he could pay up. He paid; he was forgiven. End of story.

But these were *serious* crimes. And I wanted to be the one to catch the criminal. I *love* mysteries. And what could be better than a real live one, mine for the solving? By the time the rain had stopped and the sun came out, I had assembled my team of detectives.

Sam was totally into it; she was mad at Jeremy for yelling at her gramps and swore that she'd show him by finding his stupid boat. So were Helena and Viola, and their new shadow, Max. Amanda? Not so much. She was more interested in sitting on the dock in her bikini, waiting for Patrick to come by. (He did, by the way. Come by. And, even though he should have been training for his swimming race, he spent most of the afternoon tossing Amanda into the water.)

The rest of us prowled around all afternoon, looking for clues (not that we found any) and kayaks (ditto) and talking about possible suspects (so far, just about everybody at Paradise Cottages). We may not have solved any crimes, but we had a blast.

Little did we know that our criminal had only *begun* his (her???) crime spree.

Chapter Seven

"Buenos días, Ophelia! Como estas?"

I rolled my eyes, but Poppy cheerfully ignored me.

"Como estas?" he repeated.

It's another Parker family tradition. Poppy and Mom always come to Paradise with some "project" in mind. They don't believe in estivating[7] during summer vacation. Last year Poppy was into learning to identify ferns, for example, while Mom spent her time rereading all the Greek and Roman myths. They like the family to participate, which is why I can tell a Christmas fern from an ostrich fern, and how I know the story of Narcissus. This year, Poppy is brushing up on his Spanish, which he last studied during the ice age, which is to say when he was in college. He intends to speak nothing but Spanish every morning while we're here. Mom speaks Spanish pretty well already; her goal is to learn how to do watercolors. My parents are extremely chrestomathic[8].

Okay, I can deal with that. Fortunately, I took

---

[7]estivate: the summer version of hibernate

[8]chrestomathic: devoted to learning useful things

beginning Spanish last year so I remember some stuff, enough to survive. I knew he was asking me how I was. *"Muy bien, gracias, y usted?"* I asked, using the more formal form since I was addressing an elder. (Good, thanks, and you?)

"Bien, gracias." Poppy beamed. *"Deseas tu el desayuno?"*

Since he was holding out a box of cereal, it was easy to figure out that he was asking if I wanted breakfast. *"Sí, gracias,"* I said. (Yes, thank you.)

Amanda followed my lead and just said all the same things I did. She never took Spanish, but you wouldn't know it. She's smart and picks things up quickly.

We sat down at the table with our cereal. Fortunately, Poppy doesn't remember too much more Spanish, so it was a pretty quiet meal. He studied the Spanish textbook he'd brought, and once in a while he came out with some comment like, *"llueve,"* which means "it's raining."

So it was. Just like the morning before. "I hope it clears up before our race," said Amanda.

"It will," I promised. I glanced at the kitchen clock, which is in the shape of a rooster to match the plates. "Ours doesn't start for a little while. But the first one must be starting soon. It's already nine-thirty."

Just then, we heard a loud *boom*.

41

Amanda jumped. "What was *that*?" she asked.

"Cap'n Teddy's cannon!" I said. "That means the races are about to begin!" I'd forgotten all about the cannon, but hearing it made me remember all the races of years past. Cap'n Teddy has this little brass cannon — he says it came off a pirate ship — that he just *loves* to shoot off. He uses it instead of a starting pistol. The sound echoes all over the lake, and it never fails to get me all psyched for whatever race is about to start.

"Was that the cannon?" Helena asked, coming into the kitchen, rubbing her eyes. At home, Helena's always the first one up, but she loves to sleep in when we're at the lake. Viola was right behind her.

"Aren't the little kids first?" she asked. "Max will be so bummed if we're not there!"

"*Como estas?*" Poppy asked, a little late. "*Deseas desayuno?*" He shook the cereal box hopefully.

"No time!" said Helena, grabbing a bagel from the counter.

"Let's go!" said Viola, grabbing a yogurt from the fridge.

Juliet ran in just then. "The cannon!" she said. "It went off! Time for the races!" She grabbed a bagel, too.

"*Adios,*" I told Poppy as the five of us headed out the door.

"*Adios*," he said, looking a little forlorn. I knew he'd put his Spanish book away in a moment and follow us down to the dock. Nobody wants to miss the races.

It was still misting a little by the time everyone had assembled near the dock. Patrick, wearing a yellow hooded rain jacket, was helping Rinker get the motorboat ready.

"Can I help?" Amanda asked, going right up to Patrick.

Rinker, his pipe clenched between his teeth, frowned. "Not unless you have a gallon of gas to spare, young lady," he said. He turned away, grumbling.

"He can't find the gas can," Patrick explained. "It's usually locked up in the boathouse, but it's missing."

"It was there yesterday," Rinker said. "Missing its cap, but there all the same. Now it's just plain missing."

Cap? I wondered if that was the cap I'd picked up in the ashes of the summerhouse. If so, somebody had used gas to make sure their fire burned fast and hot. That thought was a little scary.

"I've got some gas," offered Jack Carson. "Hold on, I'll go grab it." He hustled off to his little red motorboat, which was tied up at the small dock in front of Dunworkin'. His boat was named *Jack's*

Toy. He leaned into it, pulled out a red gas can, and trotted back to the main dock.

Hmm. A red gas can. Same color as the cap I'd picked up. I filed that fact away.

"Well, then!" said Cap'n Teddy, rubbing his hands together as he watched Rinker fill up the tank. He was standing on the dock, the little cannon at his side."All set now?" He glanced around. A whole crowd of people had gathered near the dock, practically everyone at the Cottages. Some were there just to watch: Mom and Poppy, who had arrived by then, and the Moscowitzes — or, at least, Annette and the babies, who were napping in a stroller. Others were obviously ready to race, including Max.

"First," bellowed Cap'n Teddy, "is the doggie paddle race. For little ones and nonswimmers."

Max was jumping up and down impatiently. "That's me!" he cried. "That's me!"

"Me, too," said Rita Carson, who was dressed in a frilly red-and-white-polka-dotted suit with a little skirt. She also had on a bathing cap that was covered in huge red rubber roses. She smiled down at Max. "Ready to race?" she asked.

Max grinned. "Ready!"

A couple of other adults had lined up: Mr. Wallbridge, who never learned to swim even though he's a good sailor, and Tessa Green's mom, who's always game for anything.

"Go, Max!" yelled Helena.

He raised his hands like a prizefighter, as if he'd already won the race.

Rinker started the motorboat and putted out to a spot not too far from the dock.

"Out to the boat and back," said Cap'n Teddy. "I'll call Ready and Set, then fire the cannon. Okay?"

"Okay!" everybody chorused. Max and the grown-ups eased themselves off the dock and into the water. (Nonswimmers don't start with a dive, obviously.)

"Ready! Set!" cried Cap'n Teddy. Then he fired the cannon. *Bang!* They were off.

It's hard to watch the doggie paddle race without totally cracking up. I'm sure everybody laughed when *I* was in that race years ago. Not that I'd have noticed. I was probably totally focused on keeping my head above water.

Max started out strong and stayed in front all the way out to the boat. He churned his hands under his chin and kicked randomly, propelling himself along at a surprisingly good speed. Rita Carson was close behind him, her red roses bobbing as she motored through the water. Mr. Wallbridge and Mrs. Green were hopelessly behind in seconds.

Out at the boat, Max reached a hand up to slap its side. "Look at me, Helena!" he yelled. "Viola, watch." He gurgled a little on that last word, as his chin dipped below the water. But he kicked a few times and got himself above water again, then started making his way back to the dock.

I'll spare you the suspense: It was neck and neck the whole way, but Max was victorious in the end. He ran right past his mother's open arms and into Viola's, then made her and Helena come with him as he went up to receive his trophy from Cap'n Teddy.

The trophies are recycled from year to year, and most of them aren't even real swimming trophies. The only one I ever won, when I was ten, was a bowling trophy with a statue of a woman in a little skirt, holding up a bowling ball. But boy, was I proud. I got to go to the common house every day and see that trophy on display, next to a little card with my name on it.

The next race was for eight- to twelve-year-olds. Helena entered, Viola didn't. The twins are very different that way: Viola is so not into athletic competition, while Helena eats it up. Sally Wallbridge entered, too, and so did Juliet.

Rinker brought the motorboat in and tied it up, since the next race went all the way out to the floating raft. Cap'n Teddy checked to see if everyone was ready. In a few moments, *boom*! The cannon went off again and the swimmers thrashed through the water. Helena was doing the butterfly stroke, which she does really well. (I've never been able to do it without looking like an uncoordinated dodo bird.) Sally and Juliet were both doing the crawl. The race was close as they headed out to the raft, but on the return leg Sally fell behind a little, leaving Helena and Juliet to fight it out.

In the end, Helena won by a nose. Max was ecstatic.

Sam, Amanda, and I were the only ones in the thirteen-to-fifteen category. I knew I didn't have a chance. Sam spends the entire summer at Paradise and swims like a fish, and Amanda is on her school's swim team. I wasn't even going to enter, but they talked me into it.

When the cannon went off, I did my best. Unfortunately, I've never totally gotten the breathing thing down, so I can't do the crawl all that well. I have to switch off between styles, starting out with the crawl, changing to the backstroke, then doing the breaststroke for a while in order to catch my breath. I was concentrating on making it out to the raft and was a little more than halfway there when I saw Sam steaming back toward me. Where was

Amanda? She was ahead of me, I knew that. But way behind Sam. Then I spotted her, stopping in midstroke to tug at her bikini bottoms.

I could have told her that bathing suit was a mistake. I knew she had a perfectly good Speedo with her; I'd seen it when we unpacked. But no, she had to wear the bikini because Patrick was going to be watching.

I honestly think she could have won. But Sam was the winner by a mile. No contest. She grinned as Cap'n Teddy gave her a big hug and handed her a trophy (with a statue of a boy swinging a baseball bat).

Amanda wrung out her hair. She didn't seem too upset about her big loss. "Good luck, Patrick," she said, walking over to watch as Patrick warmed up, swinging his arms and stretching his calf muscles.

"I may need it," Patrick said, glancing at Tessa. I followed his glance. Tessa sure did look ready to race, limbering up on the other side of the dock. She'd left her towel and dry clothes in a neat pile.

"Are the sixteen- to eighteen-year-olds ready?" Cap'n Teddy called. These racers had to do two laps: out to the raft and back, then out again and back once more.

"Ready!" answered Derek, who had just jogged

up onto the dock and pulled off his warm-up pants.

Hmm. Speaking of ready to race, Derek looked surprisingly fit for a computer guy. I saw Tessa checking him out, a tiny frown on her face. Like the rest of us, she probably hadn't thought she had any competition other than Patrick.

Cap'n Teddy got his cannon loaded.

The swimmers were poised to go.

"Ready! Set! Go!" yelled Cap'n Teddy. The cannon boomed, and the three swimmers started to knife through the water.

"Check out Derek!" Juliet said.

He took the lead right away, streaking along like an Olympic swimmer. Tessa and Patrick were working hard to stay near him.

Derek stayed in front all the way to the raft, and even for a while on the return trip. But then he must have run out of steam. He fell back, and Tessa and Patrick passed him, Patrick a little bit ahead.

The second lap of the race was a total nail-biter. First, Tessa would be ahead. Then Patrick would sprint for a while, catch up, and pass her. Then Tessa would pass Patrick again.

Amanda could barely watch. She kept squinching her eyes shut, covering them with her hands.

"I can't watch!" she'd say. "Is he winning?" Then she'd peek through her hands. "Yes!" she'd cry, if Patrick was in the lead, or "Go, Patrick!" if he wasn't.

I was rooting for Tessa myself. I've always liked her. She's never acted better than me, just because she's older.

In the end, it was nearly a tie.

Nearly.

Tessa won, by about a centimeter. Her hand slapped the dock first; I was right there, and I saw it. So did Cap'n Teddy. As soon as all three racers were standing on the dock, he handed her the biggest trophy yet. It had a hockey player on it. Everybody there started clapping and whistling for Tessa. "Congratulations," he said, pumping her hand. Then he turned to Patrick. "You did well, son," he said in a quieter voice. "Tried your best. Good job."

Patrick just grunted. He didn't look happy. When Amanda tried to hand him a towel, he brushed past her without a word and left the dock. Sam went after him.

Derek, meanwhile, was beaming. "Did you see me?" he asked his dad. "I was out front for a long time!"

Cap'n Teddy called for a ten-minute break before the adult race. Rinker headed toward the common house, probably to refill his pipe or something. Some other people drifted that way, too, until there were only a few of us left on the dock: me, Helena, Max, Rita Carson, and Susan Buxton. Max kept patting Helena's trophy and telling her how beautiful it was.

In a few minutes Cap'n Teddy called for all the adult racers to assemble. Jeremy Wilson was the first to be ready.

"I talked to him this morning," Tessa whispered to me. "Turns out he was a star on his college swim team. I think he's going to blow everybody away."

The rest of the adults lined up more slowly: Jack Carson, Steve Green (Tessa's dad), Susan Buxton, and (surprise!) my own mom were all going to race.

I have to say that out of that crew, Jeremy and Susan were the only ones who looked as if they had a chance. Mom is no athlete, even though she did play basketball back when she was in college. Jack has quite a potbelly. And Steve Green pretty much looks like your basic couch potato.

Cap'n Teddy pushed back his hat and took a look at the racers. "Everybody ready?" he asked. "You'll be racing to the raft and back."

"Ready!" they said.

"Okay, then." Cap'n Teddy bent to check his cannon. "Ready! Set!"

"Fire!" someone yelled from back on shore.

Cap'n Teddy looked confused for a second. That wasn't what came next.

"FIRE!" The person shouted it louder this time.

I turned to look back at the shore. Then I saw it. A column of black smoke, rising from behind a grove of trees.

Chapter Eight

There really was a fire.

We all took off running toward the smoke.

It was Windswept.

And, by the time we got there, it was obvious that there was no point in calling the fire department. There wasn't anything anyone could do. The cottage was totally engulfed in flames, and it was burning down more quickly than you can imagine.

We stood there watching. Nobody spoke. I could feel the hot breath of the fire on my face and hear the crackling as it gobbled up the little house. Mom, who'd ended up near me, put her hand on my shoulder as we stood there, waiting for it to be over. It didn't take long. The roof fell in, the cottage collapsed, and the flames began to die down.

Quickly, Cap'n Teddy and Rinker organized a bucket brigade. We made a line of people from the lake to the cottage and handed buckets full of water from person to person. The first person scooped water, and the last one poured it on the flames.

Before long, the fire was almost out. Wet, black-ened timbers sent stinky smoke into the air, but there were no more flames.

I stood there, staring at the rubble.

And thinking.

Chapter Nine

"Well," said Cap'n Teddy. "Well." He stood looking at the mess that was once Windswept. His face was smeared with black soot; everybody's was. He shook his head. I'd never seen him look so down. He turned to face us. "I guess that's it for the day, folks," he said. "Thanks for your help. We'll postpone that last race. Somehow my heart's just not in it now."

Sam stood between her gramps and Duchess. I could tell she was fighting back tears, but she stood straight and tall, holding her grandmother's hand. Duchess looked very sad and suddenly years older.

"Can't blame you," said Jack Carson, who was standing on Cap'n Teddy's other side. He put a hand on his friend's shoulder. "Come on, I'll buy you an ice-cream sandwich."

The two of them walked off, followed first by Rinker and then by the rest of us. I saw Mom counting heads, making sure that Helena, Viola, Juliet, Amanda, and I were all there. Then she gave me a little wave and headed down the path. Juliet and Sally took off toward the dock. I turned to Sam as we left the clearing where Windswept once sat. "This is serious," I whispered to her. "We have to figure out who's doing this stuff."

"No kidding. I *hate* seeing Gramps so sad," she said fiercely.

We grabbed Helena and Viola as they walked by. "Time for a meeting," I told them. "Coming, Amanda?"

Surprisingly, Amanda had been a big help with the bucket brigade. For a few minutes, she'd seemed more like the old Amanda, the one who was always ready to get involved in whatever was going on.

"You're not going to play detective again, are you?" she asked, wrinkling her nose. "I'll catch you later. Right now, all I want is a shower. Anyway, I have to see how Patrick is doing and all."

Old Amanda had disappeared again, and Valley Amanda had taken her place once more.

What could I say? "Later," I told her. She walked off toward our cottage.

That left four of us. "Okay," I said, facing the others. "Here's the deal. We have to figure out who could have set that fire. And we have to do it soon. Right now is the time to question everybody. It's our best chance to catch the perp."

"Perp?" Helena asked.

"Perpetrator," I explained. "The person who committed the crime. That's what they always call them on the cop shows."

Helena shrugged. "Okay," she said. "If you say so."

"I have a plan," I went on. "We divide the cottages up between us. Then we fan out and question everybody. When we're done, we meet up again and try to put it all together."

"What are we questioning them about, exactly?" Viola asked.

"Their whereabouts. Where they were during the races."

"But everybody was down at the dock!" said Sam. "I mean, I was there the whole time. Well, except for when Patrick and I went back to our cottage, just after his race. But we were together then. We were together the whole day."

"I'm not asking *you* for an alibi," I told her. "But that's exactly the kind of information we need about every resident of Paradise. *Were* they at the races? If so, were they there the whole time? If they weren't there, or weren't there the whole time, we need to account for where they were. And it's best if there's some way we can verify what they're saying. Like, the way you said that you and Patrick were together. You can vouch for each other."

Viola was nodding. "I get it," she said. "Then, maybe once we have all the information, we can make a chart or something."

I beamed at her. "Exactly what I was thinking!" I said. "Okay. I'll take our cottage, because I have to go back there anyway for a notebook and pen. And I'll do Dunrovin' and Dunworkin'. Helena, you take Dew Drop Inn and Happy Hideaway. Viola, Seventh Heaven and Bide-A-Wee. Sam, Shangri-La and Sleepy Hollow. How does that sound?"

Sam shrugged. "Fine with me," she said.

The twins nodded, too.

"Let's meet at the Poppa Bear rock in half an hour," I suggested.

We were off. I headed straight for our cottage. Mom was sitting out on the porch, so as soon as I'd found my notebook (I always have one around in case I hear a new word I have to write down) I decided to question her first. I sat down next to her and clicked my pen.

Beverly Parker, I wrote at the top of a clean page in my notebook. "So, Mom," I asked, trying to sound casual, "did you see all the races?"

"Every one," she answered, without really looking up from the watercolor she was working on. "You did very well, honey."

"Are you sure you saw my race?" Nobody who

watched that pathetic performance could say I'd done well at all.

Then she did look up. She smiled at me. "I know you didn't win," she said. "But you tried hard. That's what counts."

Right. That's what everybody always says. But it's not really so true. From what I've seen of most sports, what counts is winning. I let it go. "So, you were down at the dock all morning, right?" I asked.

She nodded. "All morning," she agreed. "Up until the fire, that is." Her face changed, thinking of that terrible fire. "I feel so bad for the Drysdales. Wasn't that awful? Anyway, after I helped out with the buckets, I came back here to wash up."

At dock for all races, I wrote. *Helped with fire.* "Well, I guess you want to get back to your painting," I said. "It's good. The pine trees look real."

She sighed. "Thanks. But I'm not concentrating all that well, to tell you the truth. That fire really shook me up."

"Me, too," I told her. We sat in silence for a few moments. Then I glanced down at my notebook. If I wanted to get all my questioning done, I had to get going.

Before I left Whispering Pines, I talked to Poppy and Juliet. They checked out perfectly: Both of them were on the dock the whole time, except when they headed up to the common house together during the break because Poppy wanted some pretzels.

David Parker: On dock all morning. Common house. Alibi supported by Juliet Parker.

Juliet Parker: Ditto. Supported by David Parker.

Amanda was in the shower, so I couldn't talk to her, but I didn't have to. She'd been pretty much in my eyesight the whole time.

That did it for Whispering Pines. On to Dunrovin' and Dunworkin'.

I passed Dunworkin' first, so I stopped to talk to the Carsons. They were on their porch, sipping iced tea and talking quietly.

"Hi!" I said. "I'm Ophelia Parker, from Whispering Pines. Sam's friend?"

"Sure, honey," said Rita. "We haven't been formally introduced, but we know who you are. We're Rita and Jack." She'd changed out of her bathing suit and was now dressed in a lilac sweatsuit. "Come sit for a spell and have some tea."

It seemed like a good way to ease into the questioning thing, so I accepted, even though I don't love iced tea. "Were you really a safecracker?" I asked Jack when he handed me a frosty glass he'd brought from the kitchen.

He laughed. "Teddy's been telling tales again," he said.

That wasn't exactly a denial. I was itching to

make a note in my notebook, but I thought I'd wait until I left. I sat and chatted with them for a while, mostly about the fire and how awful it was, and managed to get a pretty good idea of their whereabouts that morning. Finally, I took the last few sips of tea, thanked them, and headed off down the path. As soon as I was out of their sight, I stopped to make some notes.

Jack Carson: Watched wife's race. Then spent some time on porch doing crosswords, until he heard someone yell "Fire!"

Rita Carson: On dock for most of morning. Returned to cottage to change clothes. Was in shower and did not hear of fire until Jack returned from bucket brigade.

Next stop: Dunrovin'. The Drysdales. I felt a little awkward about barging in on them, since I knew they must be very upset about the fire. And it seemed obvious that neither of *them* could be a suspect. Why would they destroy their own property? But I thought it was a good idea to hear what they had to say about the fire, anyway.

I didn't get a chance to talk to Cap'n Teddy. He was down at the common house, Duchess told me, handing out free snacks to everyone who had helped on the bucket brigade. Duchess herself was very upset. "The summerhouse was bad enough," she said. "I hated to lose it. But then a boat is stolen, and now this! Can it really be a coincidence?" She paced around, clutching Brinkley tightly against her chest. As usual, she was beautifully dressed in white pants, a navy-blue blouse, and a single string of pearls. Brinkley's collar was navy blue that day, too, I noticed. I wondered if they always matched.

"Are you going to call the police?" I asked.

She shook her head. "Teddy doesn't want to," she said. "He feels it would be bad publicity for Paradise Cottages. And that's the last thing we —" She stopped herself. "Nobody needs bad publicity," she finished.

I nodded. "Of course not." I wanted to tell her not to worry, that we'd find out who had set the fires and stolen the boat. But could I really promise that? After all, I didn't really have a single clue yet, unless you counted the gas-can lid or the bent matches.

I figured I should at least ask her the same question I asked everyone else. "Were you down at the dock all morning?" I asked.

She nodded. "Oh, yes, dear," she said. "I love to watch the races." She thought for a moment. "On second thought, I wasn't there the *whole* time. I missed the second race, because I came back here for a hat. I remember, because I saw Rinker talking to Mike Buxton, over by the old summerhouse site. I believe Rinker was asking for some professional advice on rebuilding."

Interesting. That meant that neither Mike Buxton nor Rinker had been down at the dock at that point.

I talked with Duchess a little longer. Then I glanced at my watch and realized it was time to meet the others. I said my good-byes and raced over to the Poppa Bear rock. Helena and Sam were already there, and Viola joined us a few minutes later.

I took a second to write down what Duchess had told me:

Duchess Drysdale: At dock, except for walk to get hat. Saw Rinker and Mike Buxton.

Then I asked the others what they'd found out. And suddenly, I began to realize how complicated this was going to be. There weren't that many people at Paradise Cottages, but they sure did move around a lot.

Derek Wallbridge slept late and barely made it on time for his race.

Carl Moscowitz napped with the twins, then took them for a walk in their stroller. Both of them spit up and needed their clothes changed.

Sally Wallbridge went back to Happy Hideaway after her race because she'd forgotten a towel.

Susan Buxton was doing yoga on her back porch until it was time for her race.

Rinker wouldn't answer any questions. Said he was too busy for such nonsense.

And Jeremy Wilson borrowed a canoe for an early-morning paddle, then changed and showed up in time for his race.

I tried to make a chart. But when it was done, it was just a confusing mishmash of lines intersecting all over the place. The only people we could definitely clear, it seemed, were the ones who really *were* on the dock the whole time: ourselves and Cap'n Teddy.

We weren't exactly narrowing in on a suspect.

Chapter Ten

Frustrated, we all trooped down to the dock for a swim. I figured it wouldn't hurt to get our minds off the situation. All that cerebration[9] was exhausting. Besides, this *was* still my vacation! I wasn't about to let the investigation take over everything.

Amanda, now with clean, shining hair, was lying on the dock sunning herself. When she heard us coming, she turned over and yawned, adjusting the strap of her bikini. "Hey, Nancy Drew. Caught the desperate criminal yet?" she asked. I stripped down to my bathing suit and plopped down next to her, while the twins and Sam jumped into the water. I wanted to get a little warmer before I went swimming. I love the feeling of cooling off after I've been roasting in the sun.

"Ha-ha," I said. "You won't think it's so funny if *our* cottage burns down." I'd been thinking about that. So far, the person had set fire only to buildings that had fallen into desuetude[10]. But who was to say what the firebug would do next? I knew I wouldn't be sleeping all that well for the next few nights.

[9]cerebration: mental activity
[10]desuetude: disuse

"Patrick says it's probably just coincidence," Amanda reported.

Great. Now I was going to have to hear *Patrick's* opinion on everything. "But what would *Daniel* think?" I said. It was a little mean, but I couldn't help myself.

"Daniel?" she asked, looking blank.

"Yes, Daniel," I said. "Remember? Your boyfriend?"

"Like, why would he have anything to say about this?" she asked. She didn't get it.

"Never mind," I said. "But what *about* Daniel? I mean, it's like you've forgotten all about him. If you and Patrick — if anything happens between you two, isn't that cheating?"

She sat up and shook back her hair. "It's totally *not*," she said, very serious all of a sudden. "Ophelia, everybody knows that summer flings don't count. They're just, like, for fun."

"That's ridiculous!" I burst out.

She looked hurt.

"I'm sorry," I told her. "But isn't it? I mean, either you want Daniel or you want Patrick. You have to choose one or the other. Don't you?"

She shrugged. "Daniel will never know. And what he doesn't know can't, like, hurt him. I wouldn't care if *he* had a summer fling."

I didn't believe her, but I didn't want to get into

a fight. What did *I* know about this stuff? I've never even had one boyfriend, much less the prospect of two. Still, even if it was okay with Daniel, I was worried about another thing: Amanda getting hurt. Patrick's a nice guy, but I already had the feeling that Amanda liked him more than he liked her. He seemed happy to pay attention to her when it suited him, but when he wasn't in the mood — like after he lost the race — he ignored her. "Okay," I said. "Well, just be careful."

"Careful?" she asked, raising an eyebrow. "Of *what*, exactly?"

I dipped a foot into the water to see how cold it was, avoiding Amanda's eyes. "I just wouldn't want you to get hurt," I mumbled.

She made a face. "Hurt? What, you think he doesn't like me as much as I like him?"

"No, I —" It was *exactly* what I thought, but how could I say so?

"Well, for your information, he *does* like me," Amanda said. "In fact, he promised to take me out to the island later on and show me the Indian footprints."

If she'd been ten years younger, she would have added, "So there," and stuck out her tongue.

"*I* wanted to show you!" I cried, feeling ten years younger myself. The Indian footprints are one of the coolest things at Paradise. They're carved into a rocky cliff out on the island. Just the outline of footprints, six of them, walking up the rock. Some people say they're hundreds of years old and were carved by American Indians who passed through the area. (Other people say they appeared in the seventies and were carved by teenagers, but what do they know?) I really *had* been looking forward to showing them to Amanda.

Amanda just shrugged and lay back again, closing her eyes. "You never mentioned it."

Oh, well. What could I say? She wanted to go with Patrick. I looked at Amanda, lying there in the sun with her hair so shiny. "Panda?" I asked, using a nickname from way back when her dad used to call her Amanda-Panda.

She opened her eyes. "What?"

"Is everything okay? Like, with your parents and stuff?" I thought it was really weird that she wasn't talking about that at all. I mean, if you could see her e-mails. That's *all* she writes about.

She closed her eyes again. "Yeah. It's fine."

There was no mistaking her tone. She didn't want any more questions. In fact, she probably didn't want to talk anymore at all. "Well," I said, getting to my feet. "That's good." Then I walked to the edge of the dock and dove into the cold, clear water.

Chapter Eleven

"Got any real suspects yet?"

"Huh?" I shaded my eyes, looking up at the porch of Bide-A-Wee. Jeremy Wilson was sitting there, his feet up on the railing and an upside-down book on the arm of his chair. Sam was walking me back to Whispering Pines, where I was planning to do some reading myself. Amanda and the twins were still back at the dock.

"I had the feeling you girls were investigating our recent crime wave. Am I wrong?" Jeremy smiled.

"Well," I said, feeling strangely shy about it, "I guess not."

"Why?" asked Sam. "Do you have any leads?"

"Come on up," said Jeremy. "Who's your friend, Sam?"

"This is Ophelia," Sam answered. "Her family has been coming here for years."

"The Parkers," he said, nodding. "I met your dad. That's quite a kayak he built."

"He says *your* kayak was pretty nice," I told him. "I'm sorry it was stolen."

"Me, too. I'd like to know where it went!"

"It would make a good mystery story," said Sam. "A boat-stealing firebug on the loose in Vacationland."

Jeremy nodded without smiling. "It *would* make a good mystery," he agreed. "If only I knew how it ended." He paused. "I'm not convinced that the boat thief and the firebug are one and the same, though," he said.

"What do you mean?" I asked.

Jeremy gave Sam a quick glance, then turned back to me. "I've been thinking. What if the fires were set on purpose? What if they were actually arson?"

"Arson?" I kind of knew what it meant, but I wasn't sure.

"Like, what if those buildings were burned down for a reason? For example, so the Drysdales could collect the insurance money?"

Sam sat up stiffly. "What?" She turned an angry face toward Jeremy. "Are you accusing my gramps of setting fires?"

"No!" said Jeremy. "I mean, not exactly. But what if he *hired* someone to set the fires? Or what if somebody took it upon themselves to set the fires, to help him out?"

"You're crazy!" Sam stood up and faced him, her hands on her hips. "I'm not going to hang around and listen to you talk about my grandparents that way!" She stomped down the porch stairs and ran off toward the common house.

I knew I should follow her. But I was incredibly curious about what Jeremy might have to say next. So I stayed right where I was, sitting on the steps of Bide-A-Wee. "I still don't get it," I said to Jeremy. "Why would they do that?"

"To get the insurance money," he repeated. "Haven't you noticed how run-down this place is? And I know I'm paying more than you folks used to. They must have had to raise the rents because they're in financial trouble."

"Cap'n Teddy and Duchess?" I asked, thinking of Duchess's jewels. "But they're rich!"

"They *live* like they're rich," Jeremy corrected me. "I'm not so sure they really are."

"Anyway," I said, "Sam's right. It's crazy to think that Cap'n Teddy would burn down his own property!"

He shrugged. "Maybe he wouldn't," he said. "But — could you imagine Rinker doing it for him?"

I pictured Rinker's lanky form, his habit of appearing where you least expected him, the way he always did whatever Cap'n Teddy asked him to do. Plus, he had access to the boathouse, where the gas was stored. "Well . . ."

"Or what about that Carson fellow?" Jeremy asked. "I hear he has a shady past."

I'd forgotten about Jack Carson supposedly being a safecracker. "That's just a story!" I said.

"Maybe, maybe not."

I had a sudden image of Jack Carson with a red gas can. Sure, he needed gas for his boat. But what *else* was he using it for?

Jeremy Wilson was definitely getting a kick out of all of this. I could see why he might make a good mystery writer. "Any other suspects?" I asked, figuring I might as well hear everything he had to say.

He smiled. "The grandson," he said.

I gulped. "Patrick?"

He nodded. "The boy's a minor. He wouldn't be prosecuted the same way as an adult would. Maybe the grandparents talked him into it." He paused. "Or maybe he just likes setting fires. Some people do, you know."

Wow. Good thing Sam wasn't there to hear that. She would have flipped out if she heard Jeremy accusing Patrick. I didn't like it, either. I've known Patrick for a long time, and I don't think he's the criminal type. But still, I filed away what Jeremy was saying. It would be silly to ignore any possibilities this early in the investigation. And Patrick probably had access to the boathouse, too. "It's like —" I said. "Like you could think of a reason for *anybody* to do it."

"Almost." Jeremy laughed a little. "Although I can't quite figure out a motive for the Moscowitzes."

I laughed, too, thinking of those two squirmy babies and their busy parents.

Then Jeremy got serious. "Mike Buxton, now there's a different case," he said. "I find it interesting that a contractor is sniffing around like that. Especially one whose brother is one of the biggest builders in the area. They could be checking out the possibilities. Thinking about developing Paradise Cottages *their* way. After they drive the present owners away, of course."

"Whoa!" This guy had *all* the angles figured out. "You must have read a *lot* of mysteries," I said.

He laughed again. "When I'm not reading city council reports," he said. "That's my usual beat for the paper. *Bor*-ing. I read mysteries to keep my mind alert."

I could see what he meant. This conversation had definitely made *my* mind alert. By the time I said good-bye and headed on toward Whispering Pines, my head was spinning with new ideas.

Chapter Twelve

"Grab your sleeping bag! Let's go!" Sam leaped up the stairs and onto the porch of Whispering Pines. She hoisted herself onto the railing and sat there, kicking her heels.

"Go? Where?" I asked, a little groggily. I was reading a Sherlock Holmes mystery, and I was lost in a world of foggy London streets.

"The island!" Sam jumped back down off the railing. "Patrick's taking Amanda there. I figured, why not go, too, and make this the night we camp out?" She was hopping from one foot to the other, all full of energy and excitement. She seemed almost nervous.

But her enthusiasm was contagious. I put my book down and started to think out loud. "We'll need more than sleeping bags," I said. "The tent, and food for dinner tonight and breakfast tomorrow —"

"I already started packing," Sam told me. "All that stuff is taken care of. I'm telling you, all you need is your sleeping bag." Now she was actually wringing her hands. I had the feeling she really needed to get away for a bit, away from the fires and from worrying about her grandparents.

"And maybe a towel, and some warm clothes." I was still thinking. It can get chilly at night out on the island.

"Patrick said he wants to head out soon, like in half an hour," Sam urged me on. "And I'm dying to get going. Amanda's on her way back here to pack. We're meeting at the dock at four."

"My parents —"

"They'll say yes," Sam said. "You know they will. We always spend a night out there. If they let us do it when we were nine, they'll let us do it now."

She had a point. And it turned out she was right.

"Sure," said Mom when I asked.

"*Cuidado*," said Poppy. (That means "be careful.")

I threw some things into a backpack. Amanda showed up just as I was squishing my sleeping bag into its stuff sack. She'd brought one, too, so we squished together. Then she grabbed a few things, and we were off.

Patrick and Sam were waiting on the dock, next to *Serenity*, which was packed to the gunwales[11] with boxes and duffel bags. We tossed our stuff in,

---

[11]gunwales (pronounced "gunnels"): the upper edges of a ship's sides

too, then climbed aboard. Patrick started the motor and we took off.

"Yay!" cried Sam, flinging out her arms. It was good to see her so happy.

Amanda smiled into the breeze, arranging herself so her hair flew back like a model's.

Patrick looked straight out at the island, steering carefully across the smooth water.

Paradise isn't a huge lake. It took only a few minutes for us to get to the island. Patrick circled it once, just to show Amanda the whole shoreline, then turned off the engine and rowed in toward some rocks that make a natural docking spot, on the side facing Paradise Village.

Sam jumped off to tie up the boat. Then we unloaded all the stuff onto the beach. "I'll take that one," Sam said when I tried to lift a big box. She's bigger and stronger than I am, so I let her wrestle it off the boat.

"Are we going to set up the tent right here?" Amanda wanted to know.

"No," Sam said. "There are better spots over near the hut."

"Hut?" Amanda looked confused.

"There's a building on the island," I explained. "Sort of a little cabin. We're allowed to stay in it if the weather's bad, and we usually cook our meals in there. It has a stove and a sink."

"Who owns it?" Amanda asked. "Is it part of Paradise Cottages?"

"No," Sam said. "My grandparents don't own the hut or the island. They both belong to a businessman over in the village. But he lets people use them."

"Cool." Amanda went to pick up her backpack, but Patrick grabbed it first. "I'll carry that," he said. "Come on, I'll show you the hut. Then we'll check out the Indian footprints."

They took off ahead of us. Sam made a little gagging face at me, then picked up the heavy box. "She's perfectly capable of carrying her own backpack," she pointed out.

"I know," I said. "Hey, do you smell gas?"

Sam sniffed the air. "A little," she answered. "Must be the boat. Come on, let's get going!" She was still full of energy.

I guess that gas smell sort of got stuck in my nose, because I kept smelling it all the way to the hut. We made a couple of trips, until all our stuff was stowed away. Then we set up the tent and unrolled our sleeping bags inside it. We put a flashlight inside, too, so we were all set for dark. Then we set out on our usual trip around the island, checking out all the familiar spots, like the rocky place where blueberries grow and the rope swing that hangs from a tree leaning out over the water.

We decided to take a swim later, and headed for the Indian footprints.

Amanda and Patrick were there when we arrived in the little clearing, staring at the cliff. "Aren't they cool?" I asked, coming over to find the footprints and trace their outlines.

"Patrick says they're, like, really old," Amanda reported.

Like, big news.

It was hard to be annoyed at Amanda, because she seemed really happy to be getting Patrick's attention. I knew the last couple of years had been hard for her, and she deserved some good times. So I did my best to be happy for her. But it wasn't always easy that night out on the island.

After Patrick left (saying he'd be back the next morning to pick us up), she couldn't seem to talk about anything but him. She gushed about what a great swimmer he was, how good he was at driving the boat, how elegant his dive off the rope swing had been. I could tell that Sam just tuned her out after a while; in fact, Sam headed off to the hut to get dinner started and left me to listen to Amanda. I think it was just too much for her to have to listen to Amanda gush about her brother.

"And," Amanda confided in me when we were alone, "check this out. He asked me on a date!"

"A date?" I asked. "What kind of date can you

have around here?" I pictured the two of them arriving at the common house together for one of the movies Cap'n Teddy shows on an old black-and-white TV.

"We're going out for pizza," Amanda said. "On the Fourth. In Paradise Village." She kind of hugged herself, closing her eyes tight. I figured she was imagining the scene.

I wondered if she knew that the pizza place, Ozzie's, was pretty basic, with fluorescent lights, rickety tables, and a couple of stools at a high counter. "That's great," I said.

Over dinner (mac and cheese, chocolate chip cookies out of the bag), I tried to steer the conversation in another direction. "Jeremy Wilson sure had some interesting ideas for our investigation," I said.

Sam's face darkened. "Yeah, right. What does *he* know? Like, my gramps is so *not* setting those fires." She obviously thought Jeremy was guilty of ultracrepidarianism[12].

I didn't want her to get all mad again, so I skipped Jeremy's theory about Patrick. "You should have stuck around," I told her. "He had some other suspects. Like Mike Buxton." I thought she'd be surprised, but she wasn't.

[12]ultracrepidarianism: the habit of talking about things you know nothing about

"I have my eye on him," she told me.

"Patrick says —" Amanda began, but I interrupted her. I'd heard enough about Patrick for one night, and I knew Sam sure had.

"Anybody else?" I asked Sam.

Sam nodded. "I suspect Jeremy Wilson himself."

That *was* a surprise. "What?"

She smiled. "He could be desperate for a good story. For one of his books, or even for the newspaper. So he's *creating* it. See what I mean?"

"Wow." I tried to take it in. Suddenly, I saw what she meant. Jeremy had been really into this whole mystery. Maybe that was because he was its author!

We cleaned up the dinner stuff, debated whether to make a bonfire or not (*not*, we decided, since we were too tired), and snuggled down into our sleeping bags. I fell asleep almost immediately and didn't wake up until early the next morning.

Very early. It was barely light out when my eyes popped open. What had woken me up? I lay there for a minute, wondering. Then I heard it. A rustling noise — coming from the bushes nearby!

Chapter Thirteen

I peeked over at Amanda, who was sleeping on my left. She was still fast asleep, a little smile on her face. Dreaming of Patrick, no doubt.

I checked Sam, on my right. Also snoozing. One of her braids was lying over her face, so I moved it carefully. Then, slowly, I sat up and peeked out of the little screened window in the tent. I couldn't see a thing.

But I could hear something. There was definitely something — or somebody — rustling around in the bushes nearby. A bear? No, not on the island. Maybe it was just a squirrel. It rustled again. No, definitely not a squirrel. It was something bigger than that. Much bigger.

I wanted to lie back down, pull my sleeping bag up around my ears, and go back to sleep. But I knew there was no way that was going to happen. For one thing, I'd never get back to sleep now. For another, I had to pee.

Slowly, as quietly as possible, I unzipped the tent and slipped out into the misty morning air. There was a pink glow in the sky over Paradise Village; the sun was about to rise. I listened again.

No more rustling. I figured it was safe to walk over to the outhouse near the hut.

I padded along quietly, checking over my shoulder once in a while and peering around trees to see if I could spot whatever it was that was making that noise.

Whatever it was, it had stopped.

I entered the clearing near the hut and headed straight for the outhouse, a little wooden building around back.

And that's when I nearly ran into her.

Tessa Green.

"Aahh!" I cried when she came around the corner.

"Eeehh!" she cried when she spotted me.

I don't know which of us was more surprised. Tessa was in her bathing suit, and her hair was dripping wet. "Out training again?" I asked.

She nodded. "That's right. Training." She didn't meet my eyes. I wasn't sure why, but she seemed nervous.

"You're dedicated," I said. "I mean, the race is over."

"Well." She stood on one foot and then the other, hugging herself a little to try to keep warm. "Sure. But I'm a swimmer."

"So, you're just taking a break here?" I asked. "You swam out from the cottages?"

"That's right," she said again. "From the cottages."

"How long does that take?" I was impressed that she could swim so far.

She shrugged. "I don't know. Half an hour? Anyway, I better get going. My folks'll be wondering where I am."

I doubted that they'd even be up yet, but I didn't say anything. I just waved good-bye and watched her wade into the water and swim off in her indefatigable[13] way, with strong, sure strokes. Then I headed for the outhouse.

Afterward, I walked down a path and sat on a rock near the shore to watch the sunrise. It was pretty spectacular, all orange and red and pink. The sky changed constantly as the glowing ball of the sun popped over the trees that lined the lake, and all the colors were reflected in the little waves that lapped against the shore.

I was so hypnotized by what I was watching that I nearly jumped out of my skin when a canoe appeared, slipping silently through the water. I stood up fast.

"Whoa!" It was Patrick. "Caught me! I thought I could sneak up on you guys."

He was smiling, but he seemed truly surprised

[13]indefatigable: untiring

to see me. I couldn't help remembering what Jeremy had said about him. Was he up to something suspicious? Or — was he just hoping to catch a glimpse of Amanda in her pj's?

"Did you come to get us already?" I asked.

He shook his head as he climbed out of the canoe and pulled it up onto shore. "No way. The canoe isn't big enough for all your gear. Rinker's coming out later with the boat. But I thought Amanda might like to go for an early-morning paddle."

"I don't think she's up yet," I told him. "She and Sam were both totally out of it when I got up. But we can go check."

We walked back toward the hut. Sam was there, rummaging through one of the boxes we'd brought. She jumped a little when she saw us (seems like everyone was sneaking up on everyone that morning), but then she smiled.

"Pretty early for breakfast," said Patrick. "Don't you usually sleep until eleven or so?"

"Must be the island air," Sam said, closing the box and moving away from it. "I woke up hungry."

"Were you getting out the food?" I asked. "I think that's the wrong box. The bacon is in this one." I opened another box and started pulling out bacon, eggs, and bread.

By the time we had breakfast started, Amanda showed up, rubbing her eyes. She perked right up when she saw Patrick. The two of them went off for a short ride in the canoe, then came back to feast with us on slightly burnt bacon and scrambled eggs.

We were just cleaning up when Rinker arrived to ferry us back to the cottages. I couldn't believe our night on the island was already over! But we couldn't hang around much longer — not if we wanted to make it to Regatta Day.

Chapter Fourteen

"Go, Ophelia! Row! Row harder!"

That was Helena, cheering me on from the dock as I threw myself against the oars, rowing as hard as I could. Mom and Amanda, my passengers, were cheering, too. My lungs were screaming, my shoulders were crying out for mercy, and I could feel the blisters forming on my hands.

Ahh, Regatta Day.

Mention the word *regatta* to most people, and they'll picture big, beautiful white yachts sailing gracefully around a harbor. Or maybe they'll have an image of speedy, trim sailboats racing through whitecapped waters.

I think Cap'n Teddy had those pictures in mind when he organized the first Regatta Day at Paradise. But the reality here at our little lake is a bit different.

Here, Regatta Day is basically just an excuse for all of us to spend the day on the water, in whatever craft we choose. I've been known to spend Regatta Day on a rubber raft, paddling about happily, surrounded by boats of every type. Oh, there are races. That's what the word *regatta* really means: boat race. But I think the races are mostly another excuse for Cap'n Teddy to load up his cannon and fire away.

Anyway, this year I'd decided to enter the rowboat race. I was using a leaky old dinghy that belonged to the Drysdales. It was blue, or at least it used to be before most of the paint flaked off. I had to bail out four inches of water before I even got started. And the oars seemed guaranteed to give me splinters. But how could I resist the chance to win a race as skipper of the mighty *QE II*? Yes, that was the boat's name. My humble little rowboat was named after one of the biggest, most luxurious ocean liners to ever sail the high seas, the *Queen Elizabeth*.

What a laugh.

And what a gas.

The boat races are always pretty competitive, just like the swimming races. But the boat races are open not only to Paradise Cottages people but to citizens of Paradise Village as well. (Cap'n Teddy figures we go to their Fourth of July parade, so it's only polite to invite them to our Regatta Day.)

I was competing against two other rowers. Derek Wallbridge was one of them. The other was a girl from the village who looked about ten years old. Like mine, each of their boats had two passengers; it's one of Cap'n Teddy's weird rules. I was worried about Derek, but figured the girl was no threat.

Boy, was I wrong. From the moment the cannon boomed, that girl was way out in front. I could see that Derek was working as hard as I was to keep up. And he had his own cheering squad: Tessa was screaming for him to pick up the pace.

He tried.

I tried, too.

But in the end, the little girl won by at least two lengths. I'd never seen her before, and I haven't seen her since, but I'll never forget how strong she was. She deserved the trophy that day, no question.

"You did your best," said Mom as she climbed out onto the dock.

"Nice try, Ophers," said Amanda, using a nickname I hadn't heard in about five years. As she helped me tie up the boat, I saw her glance toward a row of kayaks lined up next to the dock, looking for Patrick.

Amanda had been hoping to be in the canoe races with Patrick, but at the last minute he'd switched to the kayak race. It turned out that Tessa was going to be in that race (she said it would be her first time in a kayak!), and he couldn't resist the opportunity to compete against her again. That's why Amanda ended up as my passenger.

Oh! Speaking of the kayak race: big news. Jeremy Wilson's kayak had been returned! A guy from the village had towed it over that morning behind his motorboat. The kayak had turned up at his dock one morning, and he had no idea where it came from until he saw one of Jeremy's signs (MISSING KAYAK!) at the creemee stand. Jeremy was so happy that he tried to give the man a reward, but he wouldn't accept it. When Amanda, Sam, and I pulled into the dock after our night on the island, we found Jeremy standing there, staring happily down at his trim little boat. The only damage he could find was a streak of red paint where the boat must have bumped hard against something. Naturally, he was planning to enter the kayak race, too.

Almost everybody at the Cottages was out on the water that afternoon. Dad was going to be in the kayak race, of course. So was Sam. Juliet and Sally were racing the Wallbridges' sailboat. And the twins had been talked into the canoe race; they'd be riding with Susan Buxton and Max. (Mike wasn't feeling well; according to Susan he was napping back at Seventh Heaven.)

Cap'n Teddy and Duchess were aboard their big motorboat, along with Brinkley and the cannon, and the Carsons were aboard theirs.

It was quite a scene when you looked around. The lake was full of boats, and some people had put some effort into decorating their craft with red, white, and blue crepe paper or gold streamers. There was definitely a holiday feel in the air, even though it was only July third.

"Canoe racers! At the starting line, please!" boomed Cap'n Teddy through the old-fashioned megaphone he always uses on Regatta Day.

Amanda and Mom and I rowed out toward the finish line (an imaginary line between the Drysdales' boat and the Carsons') to watch the twins compete. They were the only Cottage people in the race; the two other canoes had come from the village. One was a solo canoe, piloted by a guy who looked about Patrick's age; the other was an authentic-looking birchbark canoe paddled by a woman in a fringed buckskin dress. I've seen her before, riding a palomino in the village's Fourth of July parade.

The cannon boomed and the racers were off. The twins tried their hardest, Viola in the stern, steering, and Helena in the bow, paddling like mad. But their canoe was overloaded compared to the other two, and they didn't have a chance. The guy in the solo canoe sailed ahead and won easily. And here's the weird thing: As he crossed the finish line, he blew a kiss back toward the cottage dock!

"What was *that* about?" I asked Amanda. She just shrugged.

"Looks like the kayak race is getting under way," Mom said. "Let's row back to the dock and give Poppy some encouragement."

I let her take the oars, since my hands were still a little sore, and she rowed back toward the dock.

Poppy was joking with Tessa as he explained the basics of kayak paddling. "It's easy," he said. "The hard part is getting in and out." He showed her how to get in by straddling the cockpit and inserting one leg at a time, all the while keeping the kayak balanced. "Oops!" he hollered as the kayak tipped and sent him splashing into knee-deep water. "See what I mean?"

Tessa laughed. "I think I do," she said. She straddled her own kayak (one of the three that Cap'n Teddy keeps for customers) and gracefully stuck her legs inside.

You'd never have known it was her first time. I guess Tessa is just a natural athlete.

So, I'm not going to go into the gory details of the kayak race. I'll just tell you that Poppy didn't have a chance, but he did have a great time. Tessa and Patrick fought for the lead most of the time.

But, in the end, Jeremy won the race — and everybody was glad. It seemed fitting, since he had just gotten his boat back.

Once the races were over, my favorite part of Regatta Day began. That's when everybody pulls their boats into a big circle (usually it's just cottage people by then) and we settle in for some serious eating. Everyone has packed picnic baskets full of awesome food, and there's lots of sharing from boat to boat. You know, "I'll trade some chicken salad for some of that great-looking coleslaw." Like that. We eat until we're totally stuffed. Then we eat some more. Finally, Duchess always passes out these incredible brownies she bakes.

Then, to work off our meal, we all paddle around some more until the sun starts to go down and the stars start to pop out. That's one of my favorite times to be out on the lake. The wind dies down completely so that the surface of the water is completely calm, reflecting the stars. Everything is very quiet, except for the loons calling and the sound of soft conversation from other boats. The sky turns a deep blue, and you can just barely make out the silhouette of the trees along the shore. I always feel very content and peaceful when I'm on the lake at twilight.

Once it's dark, Cap'n Teddy calls us all back and hands out little toy boats made from a hunk of wood with a tiny sail attached. Each one has a little candle on it. We light them, make a wish, and put them in the water to sail away. It's *such* a beautiful moment. I always feel like crying.

"What did you wish?" I asked Amanda as she gave her boat a little push that night. She and I were out in a canoe together; Patrick had gone off alone in a kayak, so I guess I was her next best choice for a dinner date.

"I'm not telling!" she said. "Then it won't come true."

"That's only for birthday candles," I told her. "You're allowed to tell your boat wish."

She shook her head. "I'm still not telling."

It probably had something to do with Patrick.

My wish? Simple. I always wish the same thing. That I get to come back to Paradise *next* summer.

I looked around at the others, wondering what they wished. Poppy probably wished to go to Spain or Mexico, to try out his Spanish. And I bet Helena wished to be goalie on the soccer team this year. No doubt Mrs. Moscowitz was wishing that the twins would grow up to be strong and healthy, and —

Boom!

There was a huge explosion. I felt it down in my stomach.

I looked over at the Drysdales' boat. Was it the

cannon going off by mistake? Nope. I could barely make out Cap'n Teddy's face, but I could see enough to know he looked as surprised as the rest of us.

Boom! Boom! Boom-boom-BOOM! The tonitruous[14] sound echoed all over the lake.

Now there was light, too. It was like a thunderstorm without the wind and rain. Flashes of bright light lit up the sky as the explosions continued.

"It's my fireworks!" Cap'n Teddy yelled. "Oh, no!"

Fireworks?

"They were a surprise," I heard him tell Duchess. "I got them months ago and hid them in the hut on the island."

The hut! The island! My stomach clenched up. This was not good.

In fact, it was very, very bad.

Within moments, the worst had come true.

The island was on fire.

[14]tonitruous: like thunder

Chapter Fifteen

Flames shot into the air, mirrored by the still water of the lake. It was like a dream — no, a nightmare. How could this conflagration[15] be happening?

"Head for shore!" yelled Cap'n Teddy. "Head for safety!" He started his motor. Everybody started paddling and rowing for the main dock.

This fire was big. Much, much bigger than when Windswept burned down. The entire island was burning up, and there wasn't a thing I could do to stop it. I paddled as hard as I could, looking back now and then at the burning island as I pulled for shore. The flames grew higher and higher. I could hear the crackling of the fire and occasional loud explosions — more fireworks? The fire grew so quickly. By the time we got to the dock, even the tallest trees on the island were engulfed by flame.

"We need a head count!" shouted Cap'n Teddy. "Who's here? Who's missing?"

Oh, my God! I never even thought of that. Was everybody safe? I looked around. Amanda was

[15]conflagration: huge fire

with me. I spotted Poppy's kayak across the dock; he was just climbing out of it. I saw Mike Buxton run up the dock, coming from shore, to look for his wife and Max. He spotted their canoe just as I did. Helena and Viola and Mom were paddling hard, just coming in to the dock in our canoe. Sally and Juliet were already there. Quickly, I counted some other cottage people: Derek and his parents, Jeremy Wilson, Tessa and her parents. The Carsons pulled up in their motorboat. And the Moscowitzes were probably back at Shangri-La.

Rinker strode up the dock. "I called the village fire department," he yelled to Cap'n Teddy. "They'll do what they can."

I didn't see how they could do much. I know they have a special boat that's equipped with hoses, but I could tell just by looking at the island that it was too late.

"Where's Patrick?" cried Duchess. "Has anybody seen Patrick?"

"Patrick!" yelled Amanda. "Oh, my God! Where is he?" She stood up in the canoe, nearly tipping us over.

"And where's Sam?" I asked, suddenly realizing that I hadn't seen her, either.

We all stared into the darkness. The bright flames made it hard to see, but finally, there they were, paddling toward us in their kayaks. Patrick came first, and Sam came paddling after. As she drew closer, I could see that tears were running down her face.

"We — we were on the other side of the island," she told me, joining me on the dock after running to her gramps and gram for a hug. "It's awful! Horrible!" She was still sobbing. "Our beautiful island. The hut. Gone!"

"I know," I said, reaching out to hug her. "How could somebody do that?"

She stiffened. "Somebody? You think somebody did it on purpose?"

"I don't want to think that," I told her, "but how could all these fires be coincidental?"

She didn't answer. She just hugged me back as we stood watching the flames destroy a place we both loved.

Chapter Sixteen

I slept late the next morning. I guess I was just really, really tired.

When I woke up, the sun was streaming in through the window. Amanda's bed was empty, but otherwise everything seemed normal.

Then I remembered.

It was like being punched in the stomach.

The island was gone. Every tree, every blueberry bush, every board in the hut. Gone.

I took a deep, shaky breath — and that's when I smelled it. The smoke still hung in the air. Usually, the smell of a fire makes me feel all cozy and nostalgic; it reminds me of campfires and marshmallows and warm, fuzzy sweaters. But this time, the smell almost made me sick.

I could picture the flames leaping into the air. I could picture the way they were reflected in the water. I could picture the special fire-fighting boat that came roaring over the lake to try to put out the fire, even though it was hopeless by then.

And I could picture Sam's face, streaked with tears.

Poor Sam. I think that island meant even more

to her than it did to me! I wondered how she was feeling this morning.

I got out of bed and threw on jeans and a shirt. I had to go find Sam and see how she was doing. But when I got downstairs, I found Poppy and Mom in the kitchen, eating cereal and talking very seriously.

In Spanish.

Poppy had to keep stopping to consult his dictionary and textbook, so the conversation wasn't going so well. But I caught enough of it to know what they were discussing.

"*Es demasiado peligroso*," said Mom. (It's too dangerous.)

"*Quizá debemos ir a casa*," Poppy said. (Something about going home.)

"No!" I cried. "We can't go home! We just *got* here."

Poppy looked at me. "Ophelia," he began. Then he flipped open his dictionary and started looking something up. After a second, he flipped it closed again. "Forget it," he said in English. "It's too complicated. Look, your mother and I have been talking. We're thinking that maybe we should just pack up and go home."

"But Poppy —" I began. "Who said you had plenipotentiary[16] authority to make that decision?"

---

[16]plenipotentiary: having full power

He held up a hand. Usually, Poppy gets a kick out of it when I use big words. This time, he ignored me. "Don't you realize, Ophelia? You could have been *on* that island when the fire started."

That's when it hit me. I know it sounds crazy, but somehow, I had managed to avoid thinking about that. I had focused all my energy on feeling terrible about the island burning up. But I had never once thought of the danger. I had never once thought of the fact that the fire took place less than twelve hours after we'd left the island. And we were out there without a boat, no way to escape. "Oh, my God!" I said, covering my mouth with my hands. I sat down, hard. "Oh, my God!" I said again.

Mom got up and came over to hug me. "It's okay, sweetie," she said soothingly. "It's okay."

But it wasn't. It was awful! Was it possible — was it possible that somebody *knew* that Sam and I were investigating the fires? Was it possible that somebody wanted to scare us, or even hurt us? I shivered a little, thinking about it. Mom held me closer.

"That's okay, sweetie. We'll just go home and be safe."

Go home? Back to Cloverdale? No way! I pulled away from her. "Mom, that's not what I want."

"This isn't necessarily *about* what you want," Poppy said quietly.

I gulped. "But I'm sure the twins and Juliet want to stay, too," I said. "And Amanda. Where are they all, anyway?" I was beginning to have the feeling that there was some convincing to do, and I needed reinforcements.

"Amanda went down to the common house," Mom said. "Juliet and Sally went for an early-morning sail. And the twins are watching Max this morning so Mike and Susan Buxton can have some time to themselves."

Great. So I was on my own. I thought quickly. Arguing with parents can be a special art. If you really want something, you have to know how to go about asking for it. "What about the parade?" I asked, trying not to sound whiny. They hate whining. "Today's the Fourth. We've never missed the parade before!"

Poppy, frankly, didn't look as if he cared much. But Mom's more sentimental. I could tell that got her thinking.

"And wouldn't it be kind of rude to the Drysdales?" I tried another tack[17]. "I mean, if everybody just ditches this place on them? They'd feel terrible if everybody left."

Poppy nodded, considering that. I saw him exchange a glance with Mom.

---

[17]tack: a course of action, especially one in a series of different approaches. It's a word from the sailing world. Juliet taught me what tacking means; it's when you go back and forth trying to get the most wind in your sails.

What I didn't say, but what I was thinking, was this: *And I haven't even had a chance yet to catch the person setting the fires!*

It was time to finish up. (I've found that it's best to keep it to three points at a time. More than that and you lose track of your argument.) "Anyway, it's not like any of the fires have been set in places where people are actually *living*. I mean, first it was the summerhouse. Then Windswept, which was empty. I bet last night's fire wouldn't have been set if anyone was on the island."

I knew it was sort of a long shot, trying to convince them that we weren't actually in danger. For all I knew, our cottage could be next. But it did seem unlikely. I tried to put my own fears away. I *hated* the thought of leaving. I hadn't done any of the stuff I love to do every summer with Sam, other than sleep on the island. I didn't want to miss my whole Paradise vacation just because of some stupid firebug.

After that last argument I kept my mouth shut and watched as Mom and Poppy had one of their silent conversations, the kind they're great at. They don't say a word. It's all just eye contact and facial expressions. I guess you learn to communicate like that when you've been married as long as they have.

Finally, Poppy nodded, as if they'd come to an

agreement. Mom nodded, too. Then Poppy turned to me. "Okay," he said. "We'll stay for the parade, at least. We can all go over there together this afternoon. It doesn't seem fair to make you miss that. But after that —"

I didn't even let him finish. I just jumped up and kissed them both. "Thanks!" I said. "Thanks, thanks, thanks." Then I grabbed a bagel from the counter. "I'm going to find the others," I said as I headed out the door. Little did my sisters and Amanda know how close we had come to packing up the van. I couldn't wait to tell them how I'd saved the day.

"The parade's at four!" Poppy called after me. "Meet us at the common house at three, okay? We'll figure out who's going in which boat."

I found them all down at the main dock. Sam was sitting at the end, her arms wrapped around her knees. She was staring out at the island. It looked horrible that morning; all the trees were blackened stumps, and there were still gray feathers of smoke rising from a few spots.

Patrick and Amanda sat next to each other on the other side of the dock, kicking their feet in the water. Just as I got there, Patrick scooped up a handful of water and splashed her playfully, and Amanda shrieked and giggled. I knew she didn't really mind; it was already so hot out that the water must have felt great.

Meanwhile, Helena and Viola were playing with Max in the shallow water, wading around trying to catch minnows in an old mayonnaise jar. I remembered doing that for hours at a time when I was little. Max was totally into it, yelling, "Here, little fishies! Come here!" as he chased them around.

I went up to the end of the dock and sat with Sam. I tried to be quiet, since I could see that her eyes were still red from crying. It was like being around somebody who just had a death in the family. In a way, I guess that's exactly how Sam felt, like the island was part of her family.

But after a few minutes of respectful silence, I just had to speak up. "Sam," I said, "we have to figure out who's doing this."

She nodded bleakly.

Just then, Helena waded over and hauled herself up onto the dock. "Ophelia," she said urgently. "I have to tell you something." She glanced back at Max and Viola, who were still engrossed in the minnow game. "It's something Max said this morning."

I nodded. Of course, I had told my whole detective team about everything Jeremy Wilson and I had talked about, and I'd told the twins to keep a special eye on Mike Buxton. "Go on," I told her.

"He said that his daddy told his mommy that he

had his checkbook and his hammer ready," reported Helena. Then she giggled. "Actually, Max didn't say 'checkbook.' He said 'bookcheck.' But Viola and I figured out what he meant."

"Wow," I said. "Did you hear that, Sam?"

But Sam didn't really seem to be listening.

I turned back to Helena. "So, you think that means he's all ready to buy this place and fix it up?" I asked. That would make me extremely suspicious. Naturally, he'd be trying to get Paradise Cottages for the lowest price possible. Wouldn't the fires make it worth less? "Listen," I told her. "Just keep a very, very close eye on Mike, okay? And keep listening to everything Max says. Let's meet up again later. When are you done baby-sitting?"

"We're supposed to meet Susan and Mike for lunch. After that, we're free. So, one o'clock?"

"One it is," I said. "Meanwhile, Sam and I will poke around some more. And we're supposed to meet Mom and Poppy at the common house at three, to figure out how we're all getting over to the parade." Later, I'd tell Helena and Viola how lucky we were to even be there that day.

I nudged Sam. It was time to get her moving. She couldn't sit and stare at that island all day. "Let's go look around," I said. "Maybe we can find some clues." I got up and held out a hand. Reluctantly, she took it and let me pull her up.

I looked over at Amanda, wondering if she'd want to come with us. But she didn't even seem to see me, she was so focused on Patrick.

"Forget it," Sam said, following my gaze. "I have something to tell you, anyway."

"What?" That sounded very mysterious.

"Not here," she said. "Let's go up by Poppa Bear." She took off at a fast pace. After one last guilty glance back at Amanda (she was my guest, after all, and we'd hardly spent any time together), I followed her.

"So, what's up?" I asked, panting a little, as we leaned against Poppa Bear a few minutes later. The rock felt cool against my skin, and the blasting sun didn't penetrate through the thick trees surrounding us.

"I didn't want to scare everybody," Sam said in this very serious way, "but I think you should know. I was out early this morning, and I saw a guy."

"A guy?" What was she talking about?

"In the woods. He had a beard, and he was wearing these old, filthy clothes. I think he, like, *lives* in the woods or something." Sam nodded. "I think he's, like, a drifter."

"What are you saying, Sam?" I asked. "Do you think this guy might have set the fires?"

She shrugged. "He looked kind of suspicious,

that's all. And he could only have gotten here by coming through the woods. Why would he bother? Maybe he was living in the summerhouse and thought he was about to be discovered, so he burned it down. And then he moved to Windswept —"

"Right." It sounded a little far-fetched to me, but if there was some stranger in the woods we should definitely tell somebody. "Shouldn't we tell Cap'n Teddy?" I asked.

She shook her head. "Not yet. Let's look around and see if we can figure out where he's living," she said. "Then the police will have more to go on."

That made me a little nervous. The guy could be dangerous. But the sun was shining and I was dying to do *some* kind of investigating, so I let Sam talk me into it. We roamed around in the woods all morning, looking for footprints or snapped branches, but we didn't find a thing. We just got hot and sweaty and scratched up from pushing through the undergrowth.

Finally, we popped out of the woods near Windswept, only to find Rinker poking around in the ruins of the cottage. He looked up when he saw us, startled.

"Uh, just figuring out how much work it's going to take to rebuild this place," he offered, even though neither of us had asked. He tapped the dead ashes out of his pipe, filled it up again, and lit it. I saw him blow the match out carefully and grind it into the dirt with his boot.

Suddenly, I knew Rinker was probably not the firebug, even though he *did* act suspicious sometimes. For one thing, the way he ground out that match proved that it wasn't his "carelessness" that had burned down the summerhouse, as Duchess had thought. For another, he lit the match as if he'd been lighting matches all his life.

That little pile of matches I'd found? They were all bent, and some of them hadn't ever lit. To me, that was the mark of somebody who wasn't used to lighting matches.

In my mind, I put a light line through Rinker's name on the suspect list. I hadn't *proved* him innocent, but he didn't seem guilty.

Later, I crossed Jack Carson off, too. Sam and I spotted him acting suspiciously near the equipment shed, and at first I thought he was using his safecracker skills to break in and steal more gas. But it turned out he was using a key, and that while he was "borrowing" some gas from the Drysdales, it was just to fill up his boat so he could bring people over to the village for the parade.

That's when Sam and I gave up and went for a swim. It was too hot to think anymore.

Later, when we met up with the twins, they had nothing new to report, either. Max hadn't dropped any more clues, and from what they'd seen of Mike that day, he seemed like a normal, vacationing dad who was enjoying his time off. Also, as Viola pointed out, he had been on shore at the time the island went up in flames. It would have been difficult, if not impossible, for him to have set that fire.

Our investigation was going nowhere fast.

And if we didn't figure out something soon, we'd be headed back to Cloverdale even faster.

Chapter Seventeen

"But I want to go with Cap'n Teddy!" Helena said. "He said I could steer the boat."

"All right, then," Mom said patiently, "so you and Viola can go with the Drysdales, and Amanda and Ophelia can come with me in the canoe."

Amanda gave me an imploring[18] look. I knew what *that* meant. Patrick would be riding with the Drysdales, and Amanda couldn't stand not to be in that boat, too.

"Um, I think Amanda would like to go with the Drysdales, too," I said. "And Sam asked me to paddle over in her canoe. How about if you and Viola take the canoe, Poppy takes his kayak, Juliet sails with Sally, and Helena and Amanda ride in the motorboat?"

It was ridiculous how hard it was to figure out who was going in which boat. Everybody at Paradise Cottages was heading to the village for the parade and fireworks. Some people had already headed off, like Jeremy, who'd gone in his kayak, and Tessa, who had decided to swim. She'd dived

[18]imploring: pleading

off the dock, leaving her clothes and a towel in a neat pile on the dock so her parents could bring them over when they came in their canoe. Poppy was already sitting in his kayak, and the Moscowitzes had piled into a canoe and were halfway across the lake.

Jack Carson was just starting up his boat. He and his wife had invited the Buxtons to ride along, and Max was perched in the bow, waving goodbye to Helena and Viola even though the boat was still sitting at the dock. Mr. and Mrs. Wallbridge were riding in the *QE II*, with Rinker at the oars, while Derek paddled a kayak.

What a crew!

I smiled to myself as our little flotilla made its way to the village. Going to the parade is one of my favorite summer traditions. Sam always asks if I want to be on the Paradise Cottages float, but I always say no. I like to pick out a good spot along the parade route and just watch as everyone goes by.

Anyway, there isn't much room on the Paradise Cottages float. It's just an old dollhouse they've fixed up to look like one of the cottages, set on the back of a pickup. Cap'n Teddy, dressed in full yachting gear, waves to the crowds while Duchess, Sam, and Patrick throw candy for little kids to scramble for. WELCOME TO PARADISE, says a big sign hung on the bumper of the truck. It's the same

111

every year. This year, the only difference would be that Amanda would be on the float, since Patrick had asked her.

Paradise Village was already bustling by the time Sam and I pulled into the village dock. The floats were lining up behind the fire station, and people in costume — I saw Uncle Sam, a duck on stilts (?!), and a dairymaid — were running around trying to figure out where they belonged. The members of the kazoo band were already assembled, all wearing bright purple T-shirts with PARADISE KAZOOSTERS on the back in yellow script. They were warming up with a painfully off-key version of "The Star-Spangled Banner."

I said good-bye to Sam and walked off on my own, scouting out the perfect spot to watch the parade. Last year I sat on top of a picnic table out in front of the creemee stand, but that spot was already taken by a big family. I didn't mind. It was too hot to sit in the sun anyway. I was looking for some shade.

A few minutes later, I found the perfect spot on a little hill near the church. A towering maple tree cast a huge cool circle of shade, big enough for all the people who had already gathered beneath it. I squeezed in between a mom with a very tiny baby and a grandfatherly guy who was wearing a red-white-and-blue top hat and carrying a little flag.

"They're about to start," he told me. "Want a flag to wave?"

"Sure." I accepted the little flag he handed me. He seemed to be carrying a whole bunch of them. He gave one to the mom next to me, too, and one each to a bunch of little boys who were running around playing tag.

"Here we go!" said the mom, pointing down the street.

Sure enough, the parade was coming our way. The first thing we could hear was the kazoo band, a little more in tune now, humming "America the Beautiful."

We cheered and waved our flags as they marched past. Behind them came a whole bunch of tractors, sputtering and backfiring as their drivers inched them along. Most of them had obviously been washed and polished for the parade, and some of them were decorated with red-white-and-blue crepe paper.

Behind the tractors came the fire truck, and after the fire truck were a bunch of floats: the Little League Champs, the Paradise Dog Club, the 4-H kids on a float made to look like a haystack, and — Paradise Cottages. "Whoo! All right, Paradise Cottages!" I yelled, waving at Sam, Patrick, and Amanda. Sam was standing between her grandparents, a protective arm around each of them.

Everyone waved back, and Amanda tossed a big handful of candy as hard as she could, right in my direction. I managed to catch one Tootsie Roll, but the little boys got the rest.

After those floats, there were a few marching groups: the Veterans of Foreign Wars, old men in their clean, pressed uniforms; the Paradise High School marching band, which was pretty small, but made up for it by playing as loudly as possible; and the Paradise Preschool, each older kid pulling a wagon carrying a younger kid.

After them came some antique cars, three horseback riders dressed in full cowboy gear, and Ella Cates, the town clerk of Paradise, riding in a red Mustang convertible and waving at everybody as if she were royalty.

Next up? The kazoo band — again! The Paradise parade always goes two times around the parade route, just to make a little parade seem bigger. This time the Kazoosters were playing the theme from *Star Wars*.

I decided it was time to walk around a little. I got up, holding my flag, and headed down the sidewalk, threading my way through the spectators as I walked in the opposite direction from the paraders. I was watching for the Paradise Cottages float to come by again when I bumped right into someone I knew: Tessa Green.

She was standing near Ozzie's, the pizza place, holding hands with a cute guy who looked very familiar. He wasn't from the Cottages, though.

"Hey, Tessa!" I said, yelling a little to be heard over the marching band, which was just going by.

She turned and saw me, and I saw her face go pale. She dropped the guy's hand. "Ophelia!" she said.

Why did she look so guilty?

Chapter Eighteen

"Hi, Tessa," I said. I looked her right in the eye. "Aren't you going to introduce me to your friend?"

She was obviously hiding something. Was this guy connected with the fires? Was she trying to protect him? *Why* did he look so familiar?

"Have you seen my parents?" she asked, ignoring my question.

"Not since we left the Cottages," I told her. "Why?"

She let out a breath. "Because, if they see me with Kurt, they'll kill me," she said. She turned to the guy. "Kurt, this is Ophelia. Ophelia, this is Kurt."

That's when I realized who he was. "You won the canoe race!" I said. This must be the boyfriend Sam had told me about, the one Tessa's parents didn't like. Suddenly, it all came together. I remembered seeing him blow a kiss when he crossed the finish line. It must have been aimed at Tessa! "Do you live in the village?" I asked. He didn't look like such a bad guy. In fact, he seemed really nice. I liked the way he looked at Tessa, like he couldn't take his eyes off her.

He nodded. "At the house with the red dock," he said. "I grew up there."

I knew that house. It was in a little cove, just across from the island. "You must have hated seeing the island burn," I said, watching his face closely. Could he be the arsonist? I still felt like he and Tessa were hiding something.

He shook his head sadly. "That was the worst," he said. "I've been going to that island since I was two and my mom took me to pick blueberries."

He looked a little choked up, and I decided he wasn't a suspect.

Tessa was glancing around nervously, looking for her parents, I guess.

"That guy must have been pretty glad to get his boat back, huh?" Kurt asked me.

Tessa swung around and glared at him. "Kurt!" she said.

Something in the way she looked at him got my brain working. I thought of the red dock at Kurt's house, and the red mark on Jeremy's kayak. I thought of the way there *was* no neat pile of clothes waiting on the dock that first early morning when I saw Tessa swimming. And I thought of how she almost won the kayak race, even though she said she'd never paddled one before. And suddenly, I figured it out. "You took it!" I said to Tessa. "You took Jeremy's boat so you could visit Kurt, didn't you?"

She took a step back. "Whoa!" she said, holding up her hands.

"When I saw you that morning, before he knew his boat was missing, you had just swum all the way back across the lake from Kurt's place!"

She stared at me, openmouthed. "Wow. Not bad, Ophelia." Then she grinned. "Busted, I guess. Yep, I borrowed the boat and paddled it over to see Kurt. But when I was ready to come back, the sun was up and I knew I'd get caught and my parents would be furious. So I swam back instead. I figured we'd get the boat back to Jeremy somehow."

"And ever since then you've been swimming all the way across and back," I said, picturing that morning I'd seen her on the village side of the island.

She nodded. "It's good training." She shot a smile at Kurt. "Hey, you won't tell on me, will you?" she asked me.

"Well, no," I said, "I guess not. Jeremy has his boat back. Anyway, I'm really glad to know that you're not the arsonist. At first I thought *that's* what you were feeling guilty about."

She closed her eyes for a second.

"What, Tessa?" I asked, suddenly a little afraid. "You're *not* the arsonist, are you?"

She shook her head. Then she opened her eyes. "But I think I might know who is," she said.

Chapter Nineteen

"WHO?" I nearly shouted. Then I realized people were staring at us. "Who?" I asked again, quieter this time.

She'd turned away from me. Now she was staring at the floats going by. At that moment, the Paradise Cottages float appeared. She nodded toward it. "Patrick," she said.

"What? *Patrick?* Why him?" I watched Patrick glide by, riding on the float. He smiled as he tossed candy to a bunch of little girls who were chasing after the float. I remembered what Jeremy Wilson had said about Patrick. *The boy's a minor. He wouldn't be prosecuted the same way as an adult would. Maybe the grandparents talked him into it. Or maybe he just likes setting fires. Some people do, you know.*

"That morning I saw you on the dock? I had just swum by Windswept. And I saw something — some*body* — walking around. Somebody in a yellow hooded slicker. At the time, I didn't think anything of it. But later, when Windswept burned down, I remembered. And Patrick was wearing that very same jacket, just before the swimming races."

I couldn't think of a thing to say. I remembered the way he'd appeared out of the dusk the night the island burned down, just ahead of Sam. And the smell of gas when we unloaded the boat, the day before. He must have been preparing to set the hut on fire!

Did Sam know? Was she covering for him?

It looked bad — really bad — for Patrick.

Chapter Twenty

"I — I have to go," I said to Tessa. I nodded at her and Kurt and drifted away, walking back down the parade route in the same direction the Paradise Cottages float had just gone. I was actually feeling a little dizzy. Maybe it was just the heat; it was truly sweltering by then and very humid. I felt as if I couldn't breathe. Or maybe it was the shock of what she'd told me. I didn't want to believe it. How could it be true, anyway? Patrick had an alibi; he'd been with Sam right before both of the last two fires. Plus he was *Patrick*, the same boy I'd known practically all my life. How could he have turned into somebody who would burn down the island? The island didn't even belong to the Drysdales, so he couldn't have done *that* for the insurance money. Maybe he *did* just enjoy setting fires, as Jeremy had said.

"Ophelia! *Ophelia!*"

My brain felt all foggy, but finally I realized that someone was calling me. I looked up and saw Olivia and Miranda across the road. They were both waving like maniacs. "Over here, Ophelia!"

yelled Olivia. Her frizzy hair was wilder than ever, with all the humidity.

I waved back. The Paradise Preschool was just passing by. I waited for the little gap between them and the antique cars and dashed across the road. I threw myself into Olivia's arms. "I am *so* happy to see you guys," I said.

Olivia looked surprised. "Well, we missed you, too. Why do you think we drove all the way up from Burlington on the hottest day of the year?"

"It's not so much that I missed you," I began. No, that didn't sound right. Of *course* I'd missed them. I love Miranda, and Olivia's not only my favorite sister but one of my favorite people in the universe. "I mean, I *did* miss you. But it's also all this awful stuff that's going on."

"You mean the fire on the island?" Miranda asked. "I heard about that at the station. I was so upset!"

"Me, too," Olivia said. She hefted the big bag over her shoulder. "I brought my camera up. I bet there are some amazing images there, with the burnt trees and all. I'm hoping Mom will paddle me out in the canoe."

Olivia's a photographer. A really good one. She's studying photography in college, and she's already had a few of her pictures published in the paper.

"I don't think you're going out in a canoe any-time soon," Miranda told her, pointing to the sky.

I looked up and was surprised to see huge dark clouds gathering right overhead. I'd been so spaced out that I hadn't even noticed!

Just then, there was a rumble of thunder.

"Uh-oh," said Olivia.

"Let's head for the Rec Center," Miranda said. "We can get shelter there and talk some more."

We started walking, but before we'd even gone two steps it started raining: huge, fat drops splashing down out of the sky. Right away, there was that special smell of rain on a summer day: the mixture of fresh water and dust kicked from the streets that just tickles your nose.

A second later, the fat drops changed to wind-blown sheets of rain, driving down hard enough to hurt a little if you turned up your face. We started running as fast as we could; so did everybody else along the parade route. The marchers scattered, too, running for shelter.

The Rec Center was pretty crowded when we got there, but we pushed in and found some space under one of the baskets in the gym. We were soaking wet, but it was warm and cozy inside. People were laughing and talking as they wrung out their hair, cleaned their glasses, and squeezed water out of their clothes. The gym felt as steamy as a jungle. The windows rattled as thunder cracked and rolled outside, and flashes of lightning streaked past the high windows.

"Listen, you guys," I said as soon as we were a little less sopping, "it's not just the fire on the island. There have been other fires, too. The summerhouse, and one of the cottages."

"Wow! Which one?" Olivia asked.

"Windswept."

Her mouth fell open. "I always *loved* Windswept. I thought it had the most romantic name. And I liked the way it sat out there all by itself."

"Exactly what might have made it attractive to an arsonist," said Miranda, thinking out loud. She wants to be a detective on the force someday; I know she'll be a great one. "So, who are the suspects?"

She knows me. Since I love mysteries, she figured I was already on the case. "Just about everybody at the Cottages!" I said. "But I haven't had any really strong suspects until —" I looked around. "I just heard something," I said in a lower voice. "There's some evidence — just hearsay[19] so far — that Patrick might be involved."

"Patrick?" Miranda asked. "Little Pat Drysdale? But isn't he only, like, seven?"

---

[19]hearsay: a report from someone else

I shook my head. "Patrick's sixteen," I told her. She might remember him as a little kid, but Patrick was plenty old enough to be starting fires.

"I can't imagine Patrick being dangerous," said Olivia.

I couldn't, either. But suddenly, I realized that he might be. And he had a date, that very day, with Amanda! For all I knew, the two of them were already at Ozzie's, ordering pizza. "You know what?" I said. "I think I should find Amanda and Sam and let them know about this."

Miranda nodded. "That's fine," she said. "We'll come with you. Looks like the rain stopped, anyway." She waved at the window. Sure enough, the sun was already out again. Summer-afternoon storms in Vermont can be intense but very short. "While we're looking, you can tell me about the other suspects. I'll make a list and call the station to see if any of them have records." She pulled a notebook out of her pocket and flipped it open. Miranda is always prepared, even when she's off duty.

We headed down the street. Water was still running down the sides, but the hot sun was making steam rise from the asphalt. As we walked, Olivia took pictures of the crowd and I told Miranda about Jeremy Wilson's ideas — and about Sam's ideas about Jeremy Wilson. I mentioned Jack Carson and Mike Buxton and Sam's drifter and Rinker.

"Rinker?" she asked. "We never *did* figure out whether that was his first or last name, did we?"

That cracked us all up. We were still laughing when we ran into Sam and Amanda, who had just stepped out of the firehouse. Amanda was trying desperately to fluff up her wet, flattened hair, while Sam squished along in her waterlogged clothes.

"Hey, Miranda! Hey, Olivia!" Amanda was happy to see both of them. They were like older sisters to her, too, when we were growing up. Sam knows them, too, of course, but not as well. After everybody had said hi, I sat my friends down on a bench for a minute and told them what Tessa had told me. I didn't tell them about Tessa taking Jeremy's boat; I'd promised to keep that a secret. I just said she'd been out swimming early one morning, and —

"*Patrick?*" Sam asked, her voice rising. "Are you crazy? I don't know why you want to make him a suspect. First you listen to what that stupid Jeremy Wilson says, and now this." She was furious. "Why don't you listen to *me*? I *told* you it's that drifter guy. I *told* you Patrick and I were together, both times."

"Sam, I'm not saying he's guilty. I'm not even saying I believe he's a suspect. But we can't rule anything out!" I felt like I was pleading with her. I couldn't stand seeing her so mad at me. I knew it must be upsetting to hear something like that about her brother, but detectives have to be objective. You can't let emotions get in your way, if you want to solve a case.

Amanda still hadn't said anything. She was just standing there, looking shocked. Then she turned on me. "I don't believe you!" she shouted. Her face was red, and her tangled wet hair shook as she yelled. "You're making it up, aren't you? Just because you don't want me to like him. You've been against us getting together the whole time!" She spun around and stalked off. Then she spun around again. "I have to go," she said, pronouncing every word very carefully. "I have a date."

Chapter Twenty-one

I watched her go. If our friendship wasn't already in trouble, this would have done it. As it was, I wondered if we'd ever be able to patch things up. "Amanda," I said, just whispering the word as she disappeared around the corner.

"She's seeing Patrick?" Miranda asked. She'd put two and two together pretty quickly.

I nodded. "They're having pizza at Ozzie's," I said. "At least, that was the plan."

"Well, why don't *we* go grab a slice, too?" Miranda was already walking that way, following Amanda.

"I'm not hungry," Sam said, crossing her arms. She sat on the bench, unmoving. "You just want to watch Patrick, see if you can catch him lighting matches or something."

"It's not that," I said. But it was, sort of. Also, I couldn't help being the tiniest bit worried about Amanda. If Patrick really was setting the fires, maybe he was a little unbalanced. She shouldn't be left alone with him, should she?

"Come on, Sam," said Olivia. "I'm buying. How does extra cheese and pepperoni sound?"

"Please, Sam?" I asked.

"Oh, all right." She got up slowly and stuck her hands in her pockets. "But if I catch you treating him like a criminal —"

"We *won't*, Sam," I promised. "I just want to be there. Anyway, aren't you kind of curious? We'll be able to spy on Patrick and Amanda's first real date."

"Oh, yeah," she said sarcastically. "Like, I'm so fascinated." But she came.

The three of us caught up to Miranda just as she was walking into Ozzie's. The place was packed, which wasn't surprising. There aren't too many places in Paradise to get something to eat, and Ozzie's makes really good pizza. Still, most people just go straight to the counter to order a slice, and then take it back outside to eat. You can usually find a seat at a table, if you're patient.

I spotted Amanda and Patrick as soon as we came in. They were sitting at a tiny table near the counter, staring into each other's eyes. Somehow, Amanda had managed to fix up her hair since I'd last seen her; she'd lost that drowned-rat look, anyway.

The smell of tomato sauce and garlic made my mouth water, and I suddenly realized that I was starving. My stomach rumbled as I looked around the room, trying to find a table we could grab.

"Over there!" said Miranda, pointing at a family that was just getting up from a table near Amanda and Patrick's.

"I'll grab it," said Olivia. "You guys order." She went over to claim the table, and the rest of us went to wait in line at the counter.

By the time it was our turn, I was hungrier than ever.

"Hi, can I help you?" The girl behind the counter was smiling at me.

"Definitely," I said. I couldn't help smiling back. She was pretty, with long dark wavy hair and striking blue eyes. Her diastema[20] only made her even more interesting-looking. "I'd like a slice with extra cheese and, um, mushrooms."

"Got it," she said, making a note on an order pad. "Who's next? Oh, hi, Sam!"

"Diana!" Sam said. "I haven't seen you all summer."

"I've been working hard," said the girl. "Hey, let me ask you something. Who's that girl with Patrick?" She cut her eyes toward Patrick and Amanda.

"That's Amanda. She's staying at the Cottages," Sam said. "With Ophelia." She gestured at me. "Ophelia, this is Diana."

[20]diastema: a gap between teeth

Diana smiled at me again, but her eyes weren't smiling this time. Just her mouth. "So, your friend Amanda," she asked me. "Is she —"

Just then, a woman behind us in line cleared her throat. "People are waiting, you know," she said.

"Oops," said Diana, ducking her head. She picked up her pen again. "What'll it be, Sam?" she asked.

Sam ordered a slice with pepperoni, and so did Olivia. Miranda got the veggie special. Diana gave our order to the guy behind her. "Talk to you later," she whispered to Sam. Then she turned to the next customer. We got sodas out of the cooler and went back to our table to wait for our slices. They came a minute later, all piping hot and greasy and gooey. Yum. I took a huge bite. "Ow! Hot!" I said, fanning my mouth. I put the slice down to cool for a second.

Patrick and Amanda were still deep in conversation. She was gazing into his eyes, but I noticed that his gaze was shifting. He was seated facing the counter; Amanda was facing away from it. Patrick would look at Amanda for a little while, then flick his eyes over to Diana behind the counter. Amanda didn't seem to notice.

Then I saw Diana, between customers, look back at Patrick. The expression on her face was unmistakable. She was hurt. And jealous.

"Sam." I nudged her. "Who *is* that girl, Diana?"

She shrugged. "Just a girl from the village," she said. "Patrick and she —" Suddenly, she put down her slice and covered her mouth. "Oh, my God."

"What?" I leaned forward, and so did Miranda and Olivia.

"I am *so* dense," she said. "I can't believe I didn't figure this out before."

"*What?*" Olivia asked this time.

"Patrick's just *using* Amanda," said Sam. "He wants to make Diana jealous. They've liked each other forever. But last year she barely talked to him. She had this other boyfriend. So now he's trying to get back at her. He's still crazy about her, I can tell. They're always playing games like this. Ever since they were little, they've been torturing each other." She watched Patrick, who, it was now totally obvious, was watching Diana's every move.

I knew in an instant that Sam was telling the truth. Suddenly, my pizza didn't look so appetizing anymore. Poor Amanda! Patrick had been working up to this pizza date the whole time. Did he really like her at *all*? I couldn't believe he'd be such a jerk.

Of course, I didn't want to believe he would go around setting fires, either.

But he might have.

I took a few more bites of my pizza, which wasn't quite so molten anymore, and looked over at Patrick and Amanda again. One more time, I saw his eyes go to Diana. This time, he actually winked!

And this time, Amanda saw it. How could she not?

Her mouth fell open. She turned in her seat and saw Diana, who couldn't hide the smile that wink had produced. Then she turned back to stare at Patrick. She knew. I saw it in her eyes. Amanda might have been *acting* like a dope lately, but she is anything but stupid.

Her face turned red. She balled up her napkin and threw it at Patrick. Then she jumped up and marched right out of Ozzie's.

Chapter Twenty-two

"Amanda!" I left my pizza and soda on the table and ran out of Ozzie's, shooting a nasty glance at Patrick as I passed by him. "Wait up!" I called.

Amanda was striding down the street, threading her way through the crowds that still lingered on the sidewalk. Nobody had left town; they were waiting for dusk, when there'd be fireworks.

I ran to catch up with her. "Come on, Amanda," I said, panting a little, when I was right behind her. "Talk to me."

She turned to face me. Her eyes were full of tears. "Oh, Ophelia," she said, "I feel like such a jerk."

I held out my arms, and she let me hug her. I felt her shoulders shaking. "It's okay," I said. I patted her hair. "It's okay, Panda."

She stepped back and shook her head. "No, it's not," she said. "I was an idiot. I can't believe I actually thought he liked me. How could I be so stupid?"

"First of all, I think he *does* actually like you," I said. I'd seen them together, laughing and talking. I really couldn't believe it was all a fake on Patrick's part. After all, Amanda was pretty and smart and fun to be with. "You're pretty, and smart, and fun to be with," I said out loud. "You can't help it if you're not Diana. He's obsessed with her. Always has been, according to Sam."

"That's her name?" Amanda asked, sniffling a little. "Diana?"

"Yup." I smiled at her. "And second of all, you're *not* stupid. Or an idiot. You just — wanted to be liked."

She nodded, sniffling some more. "Still," she said. "He *was* a total jerk. Using me that way."

I couldn't disagree.

"And if he did that," she said, "maybe he *is* capable of setting a bunch of fires. I mean, he can't *prove* he was in the common house when that cottage burned down." She turned to me, and I saw that she'd stopped crying. "Ophelia, if he *is* the one, I want us to catch him. I want him to *pay* for what he's done."

I wasn't sure whether she meant the fires or breaking her heart, but it almost didn't matter. There were two other things I knew for sure: I had my friend Amanda back. And she had joined my team.

Chapter Twenty-three

Speaking of which, it was about time for a team meeting. It was getting late by then; dusk would be falling any minute, and as soon as it was dark the fireworks would begin. Would the firebug use the opportunity to set another fire? I had a creepy feeling that we hadn't seen the end of the destruction — unless we could catch the criminal before he (or she) acted again.

"Let's find the others," I told Amanda. "We have to make a plan."

We headed back to Ozzie's. Amanda wouldn't go in, but I stepped inside just far enough to wave to Miranda, Olivia, and Sam and give them the signal to meet us outside. Patrick was leaning against the counter, chatting with Diana. I was glad Amanda didn't see that.

"What's up?" asked Sam when she and my sisters came out of Ozzie's.

"Time for a meeting," I said. "We have to crack this case *now*, before there's another fire."

Sam nodded. "Where are Helena and Viola?" she asked. "We'll need them, too."

"I bet they're already up on the hill," said Olivia.

"They always like to get a good spot for watching the fireworks."

I knew she was right. The hillside in back of the Paradise Elementary School always started filling up around this time, since it was the best viewing spot. The fireworks would be set off from a raft floating on the lake, by the village beach. We headed to the school, hoping to find the twins.

I spotted them as soon as we crossed the baseball diamond. They'd grabbed an excellent spot, on the highest part of the hill. Fortunately, Mom and Poppy were there, too. They could save the spot for all of us. I waved to Juliet and Sally, who were sitting off by themselves.

"Did you eat?" Mom asked when she saw us. She held up a covered container that I knew was filled with her famous potato salad. I was still a little hungry, but there was no time to eat right then.

"We had pizza," I answered. Then I turned to Helena and Viola. "Want to walk around a little before the fireworks?" I asked them. "We're having a meeting," I added in a whisper.

"Save our spot!" Helena told Mom and Poppy as she and Viola got up to follow us back down the hill.

We gathered near the swings in the playground.

"Okay, everybody," I said. "This is it. It's time to get serious about figuring out who's setting the fires. We need to check out all our prime suspects *now*, since there's a good chance the firebug is all set to act again. So, who wants to do what?"

Helena was nodding. "Viola and I can keep an eye on Mike Buxton," she offered. "I saw him go by just a little while ago. We'll find him and follow him."

"Good," I said. "Sam?"

"I've been meaning to tell you," she said. "I think I saw that guy — the drifter? He was over by the library when the parade went by. I spotted him from the float, but I couldn't exactly get off and follow him. I'll see if I can find him now."

Miranda nodded. "Good idea," she said. "I'll make that call to the station to see if any of the suspects have records."

"I'll prowl around with my camera," Olivia suggested. "Maybe I can catch someone in the act. A picture would be the proof we need."

Then Amanda spoke up. "I'll follow Patrick," she said.

"Oh, no, you won't," I told her. "You're way too emotionally involved. How can you be objective when you're so mad at him?"

Sam was nodding. "Ophelia's right. That wouldn't be fair. Anyway, nobody has to follow Patrick. He's innocent, and I know it."

I reached out to touch her shoulder. "I know you

believe he's innocent," I said. "And you're probably right. But we still need to check him out, after what Tessa told me."

"Whatever," she said, shrugging off my hand. She was mad at me, I could tell. But I knew I was doing the right thing.

I turned back to Amanda. "I'll follow Patrick. Why don't you try to find Jack Carson?" I suggested. "We still need to keep an eye on him. And maybe Jeremy Wilson, too."

"Whatever," she said, echoing Sam. She was mad at me, too. How did *that* happen? I never set out to make my two best friends angry. All I was trying to do was solve this case.

By the time we split up, the sun was starting to set. Fireflies were flying by, blinking their greenish lights off and on, and little kids were running around with light sticks in luminous red, yellow, and blue. The Kazoosters were still at it, performing a medley of patriotic songs for the gathering crowd. On any other Fourth of July, I would have been sitting high on the hill, eating Mom's potato salad and anticipating the fireworks. But this year, I had a job to do. "Okay, everybody. Check back here in" — I pushed the button that lights up my watch — "half an hour?"

When we split up, I headed back to Ozzie's, hoping Patrick would still be there. I was in luck!

Just as I came up the street to the restaurant, Patrick and Diana stepped outside. She must have just finished work.

I ducked into a doorway so they wouldn't see me, then peeked out to see which way they were walking. They were moving away from me, so I followed them, sticking close to the buildings so I could hide again if they happened to turn around.

Patrick had his arm around Diana, and she was looking up at him and laughing as they walked. I guess they had a truce on "torturing each other," at least for a little while.

I kept following them as they walked up Main Street. They were walking in the opposite direction from everybody else on the street; most people were headed up to the hill for the fireworks.

Main Street pretty much ends in the lake. The dock there is the one where Patrick had met us just a few days earlier. So much had happened since then! I was thinking about all of it when I suddenly realized that Patrick and Diana had stopped, about a half a block from the lake. There weren't any more stores at that end of Main Street, just houses with big, overgrown yards. They were standing underneath a tree, and it looked as if they were saying good-bye. I got as close as I could, ducking from bush to bush. I strained to hear what they were saying, but I caught only a few words.

". . . only take a few minutes," Patrick was saying.

"I'll find us a place," Diana told him. I figured he had an errand to do, so they were arranging to meet on the hill. It all seemed totally innocent so far. I was beginning to wonder if I was wasting my time. Maybe I should be helping Sam find the drifter instead. But I decided to stick it out. My legs were cramping a little from staying in one position, so I shifted a bit, hoping my bush wouldn't rustle and give me away. Then I settled in to listen some more.

I didn't hear anything for a while. Then Diana's voice rose in a question, and I could hear only two words of Patrick's answer. But I heard those loud and clear. "Whispering Pines," he said.

The name of our cottage.

My blood ran cold. (*Love* that expression. It may be melodramatic, but it really does describe what happens when you get a shock like that one.) Was *that* Patrick's "errand"? To burn down Whispering Pines? Was Diana in on the whole thing?

Chapter Twenty-four

It was nearly dark by then. The sun had set in a blaze of gold and red and pink, but I'd hardly noticed; I was too busy watching and listening.

I followed Patrick as he headed straight for the dock.

I saw him walk out to where *Duchess* (the boat, not the person!) was tied up. He threw a leg over the side, grabbed something from a spot near the motor, and jumped back out onto the dock, carrying it.

I took one step closer, squinting. What was he holding?

Then he turned to walk back toward me, and suddenly there was no question.

It was a red gas can.

Chapter Twenty-five

I didn't stop to think.

Now that I look back, I realize that it was stupid, what I did.

You don't confront a criminal on your own.

At the end of a dark street.

But, at the time, I didn't even think about it. I just stepped out of the shadows and spoke up. "What do you think you're doing?"

Patrick looked around and saw me. "Hey, Ophelia," he said, smiling. "What are you doing down here?"

"I could ask *you* the same question," I said, putting my hands on my hips.

He laughed. "I guess you could. And I'd tell you that I just came down to get this gas can. I told Gramps I'd fill it up, and I almost forgot. Fontaine's is going to close in a few minutes."

Fontaine's is the one gas station in the village.

I kept my hands on my hips. "Look, Patrick," I said. "Forget the gas. It's all over. I know what you've been doing."

He gave me a quizzical look. "What I've been doing?" he repeated.

"I understand that you're trying to help your grandparents," I said. "But if you think you can't get in trouble, you're wrong. What you're doing is a crime."

He held up the gas can. "Getting gas?" he asked. "How is that a crime?"

"It's a crime," I said, taking another step toward him, "when you're using the gas to start fires." I glanced over my shoulder, hoping against hope to see Miranda, or Olivia, or *anyone* who could back me up. That was the point when I began to realize that what I was doing was maybe not so brilliant. "And when you're about to burn down *my* family's cottage."

Patrick shook his head. "I haven't set any fires," he said. "What are you talking about?" He seemed more confused than angry.

"I'm talking about the summerhouse," I told him. "And Windswept. And the island. And then you just said something to Diana about Whispering Pines. Is our place next?"

He shook his head again. "Look, Ophelia. I was just telling Diana where you — and Amanda — are staying. I don't know how you can think I —"

"Tessa saw you!" I burst out. "In your yellow raincoat, early that morning. When you were out preparing Windswept for being burned to the ground."

There was a momentary silence. Patrick was staring at me. "That wasn't me," he said slowly. "I was home in bed that morning. I slept late on purpose, because I had the race later on."

There was something in his voice. Something strange.

"So who —" I began.

Then I stopped speaking. We stared at each other. Patrick's eyes were wide.

And I answered my own question.

Chapter Twenty-six

"It can't be *Sam*," I said at the same moment as I realized that it probably was.

Patrick sat down suddenly, the gas can at his side. He put his head in his hands and let out a little moan. "I wondered," he said. "She's been acting strange lately. She'll hardly talk to me. She says I don't care about Gramps and Gram."

"Let me ask you something," I said. I had just remembered something Amanda had mentioned, about how Patrick had been at the common house when Windswept caught fire. That didn't jibe with what Sam had told me that day. "Where were you when the cottage burned down?"

"At the common house," he said. "I remember, because I had just grabbed an ice-cream sandwich. My race was over, and I was starving because I was too nervous to eat before it."

I nodded. So he wasn't back at the cottage with Sam, as she had said. Her alibi, which covered both of them, had been a lie. "And what about when the island burned down?" I asked.

He looked down at his shoes. "I was here," he said finally. "During dinnertime, I paddled over to visit Diana for a few minutes. Then I was going to paddle right back for the candle ceremony. Only that's when the island —" His voice cracked. "Anyway, I was paddling back as fast as I could, after those first explosions. That's when I caught up to Sam. She was on the village side of the island. We paddled together the rest of the way."

Once again, the alibi Sam had supplied for both of them contained a lacuna[21]. "One last question," I said as gently as I could. Patrick still had his head in his hands. "Does Sam ever borrow your yellow raincoat?"

He took his hands away from his face and turned to look at me. "All the time," he said softly. "All the time."

[21]lacuna: a missing part, a gap

Chapter Twenty-seven

Patrick came with me to find Sam.

We walked through the dark streets of the village, watching for her in the crowds that surged toward the hill.

I wondered about Sam's drifter. Was he completely chimerical[22]? I groaned. I couldn't stand the thought that Sam had set the fires.

Sam.

My best summer friend. The one I thought I knew so well. Suddenly, it seemed as if I didn't know her at all. How could the Sam I knew, the one who skipped rocks and picked blueberries until her fingers were purple, how could *that* Sam light the match that would burn down the island we both loved so much? All this time, I had thought she was covering for Patrick. But she wasn't. She was covering for herself.

The more I thought about it, the more I became convinced I was right. I remembered the bent matches: Sam never *could* light a campfire out on the island. And the way she was so defensive

[22]chimerical: imaginary

about her grandparents, like a mother bear protecting her cubs. Then there was that gas smell when we unloaded the box on the island — and the way she had insisted on carrying one certain box herself. Not to mention the way she'd jumped when Patrick and I walked into the hut that morning as she was unpacking that same box. How could I *not* have seen it all? How could I have been so blind?

"There she is!" Patrick said, pointing into the crowd.

I spotted Sam's braids. I gulped. How was I going to find out the truth?

"Hey!" she said, waving when she saw us. "I saw the drifter! He's walking around looking really, really suspicious. But I just lost him in the crowd."

"Sam," Patrick said.

She didn't seem to notice. "He's all furtive and stuff," she went on. "Like, he's checking all the time to see if somebody's following him. I had to stay back so he wouldn't —"

"Sam," Patrick said again. "Ophelia and I —"

"We have something to ask you," I broke in.

Sam stopped talking. She looked from Patrick's face to mine. Even though it was almost completely dark by then, I could tell that her face had turned pale. "What?" she asked.

Just then, there was a loud *BOOM!* as the first of

the fireworks went off. I glanced up to see a trail of blue stars flickering overhead.

"It was you, wasn't it?" I asked. "Why, Sam? Why did you do it? *How* could you do it? The island?" I wasn't making any sense, and I knew it. I had meant to present my case in an organized way, confront her with the evidence: the borrowed raincoat, the bent matches, the false alibis. But it all flew out of my mind when I was standing there near her. Near my friend.

Sam's shoulders collapsed. She looked down at the ground. And when she looked up, I could see that she was crying. "I didn't mean to!" she said. "I didn't *mean* to burn down the whole island!"

"Oh, Sam," I said, stepping forward to hug her. Another *BOOM!* shook the air around us as she cried into my shoulder. Patrick looked on helplessly.

"I just wanted to help Gram and Gramps," she said after a little while. "That's all." She wiped her face with her sleeve. "So I set the summerhouse on fire. It was about to fall down anyway. I thought they could get the insurance money, and it would help save the Cottages. They're going bankrupt, you know," she told me.

Patrick nodded in agreement.

"I didn't know," I said softly, stroking her shoulder. Fireworks were going off one after the other now, first a shower of red, then green, then blue and sparkly white. But I barely heard the booms. I was listening to Sam.

She sniffed. "But then I realized it wasn't enough. The insurance money wouldn't even begin to pay for everything we needed to do. So I burned Windswept. I hated doing that! I *hated* it! Windswept was always the coolest cottage. But it was falling down, too. They were never going to have the money to fix it." She drew a long breath.

"And the island?" I asked as gently as I could.

She started crying again. "It was like I *had* to do it," she sobbed. "Everybody was talking about how Gram and Gramps were probably burning down their own property to get the insurance money. So I thought, if there was a fire at the hut, that would prove it wasn't them. 'Cause the hut's not their property. You know?" She gave me a pleading look.

What could I say? It made some kind of crazy sense. "I know, Sam."

"I brought the gas can out when we stayed there. Then I snuck back to light the fire, after the boat races. But then everything went out of control," she said. "I didn't know the fireworks were in there. I ran for my boat — there was nothing I could do — I was so scared!" She started sobbing again, and I hugged her close. Patrick stepped in, too, and started rubbing Sam's back.

Miranda got there just in time to hear Sam's last few sentences. Just then, the grand finale went off. Gigantic, glittering flowers bloomed overhead, lighting our faces with their shimmering brilliance, and the booms were like continuous thunder. I held Sam tight and met Miranda's eyes in the light cast by a silvery shower of sparks. There was a question in hers. I nodded slightly, to give her an answer. We had caught our firebug.

Chapter Twenty-eight

"And how would you like your burger, young lady? Medium? Well done? I've got a perfect medium-rare, just waiting for someone!"

Cap'n Teddy beamed at me. He was dressed in a white apron that said, in big cartoony red letters, KING OF THE GRILL. And he'd traded his yachting cap for one of those floppy white chef's hats. It was the next day. He and Rinker had set up a huge grill out in front of the common house and invited everyone at the Cottages to a picnic.

I smiled back. I knew his happy-host act was just that, an act. I knew he was incredibly upset about what Sam had done — and about what would happen to her. Earlier that day, he'd stopped me as I was walking past the common house. He thanked me for helping to figure out who'd been setting the fires, and for being a good friend to Sam. He was pretty choked up and emotional then. But now he was back to being Cap'n Teddy, jovial host of Paradise Cottages. It's what he does best.

"Medium-rare would be great," I said, holding out my plate. I'd already grabbed a bun, some coleslaw, and a deviled egg. Duchess and Sam had spent the whole day in the kitchen, cooking up a storm.

Sam? Yes, Sam was at the Cottages. Miranda and I had gone with her to the Paradise police, and Sam had turned herself in. After they'd gone through the whole arrest procedure — she even got finger-printed! — the police released her into the care of her grandparents. Miranda's best guess was that Sam would end up getting put on probation and sent for counseling. I was so glad that she didn't have to go to jail. I guess Sam was glad, too, but it was hard to know. She wasn't talking much, or even making eye contact. I think she was feeling totally overwhelmed. I sensed that she was mostly just relieved the whole thing was over. "No more fires, Ophelia," she said to me as we rode back across the lake that night in the Drysdales' boat. "No more fires." She looked very, very tired.

Speaking of friends, Amanda joined me just then. She had a plate full of food, too. "Let's go eat on the dock," she suggested. "It's too nice out to sit inside." Most of the grown-ups were seated at ta-bles in the common room, but Amanda was right. It was a gorgeous evening, the kind I always pic-ture when I think of Paradise. The sky was sap-phire blue, and the first stars were just beginning to twinkle. A crescent moon shone in their midst, just a tiny fingernail of silvery light. There was a soft breeze, perfumed with the scents of lake water and pine trees, and you could hear little waves lapping on the shore.

Too perfect.

It had been a beautiful day, too. Hot, but not as muggy as the day before. Just a crystal-clear blue sky and lots and lots of sun. Amanda and I had spent the whole day doing "Paradise things." She hadn't said a word about Patrick, or Daniel, or any other boy, and she hadn't used the words "hottie" or "as if!" all day. It was like being with the old Amanda. We dove off the dock and swam to the raft. We picked blueberries and brought them home to Mom, who'd made a pie to bring to the picnic. We walked through the woods, and I showed her all the old familiar landmarks. We built fairy castles, tiny palaces made out of moss and twigs and leaves. It was a perfect Paradise day, only Sam wasn't there with me.

Amanda even talked a little about her parents and the divorce. That was hard, since I hate seeing her sad. But it was good, too. For one thing, it made me see that her whole Valley Amanda act was just that, an act. Something to distract her from having to think about the real pain in her real life.

I thought about that. If I'd learned anything from this week on the lake, I'd learned this: Things are not always what they seem.

Anyway, that day at Paradise, Amanda's problems seemed far away. She seemed really happy.

"Patrick apologized to me," she told me now as we ate our burgers out at the end of the dock. She'd taken off her sneakers and she was letting her feet dangle in the cool water. "Just now, when I was getting a soda."

"What did he say?"

She shrugged. "He just said he was really sorry he'd hurt me, and that I didn't deserve to be treated the way he'd treated me." She kicked the water, sending up a little splash. "And he said that I was wrong if I thought it meant he didn't really like me. He said I was one of the nicest, prettiest girls he'd met in a long time, and that if it weren't for Diana . . ." She looked over at me with a little smile.

"Yay, Patrick," I said. "I knew he wasn't a total loser."

"Hey, you guys!" Helena was yelling at us from the shore end of the dock. "Come to the common house! Cap'n Teddy says he has an announcement to make, and he's handing out free ice-cream sandwiches!"

I popped the last bite of burger into my mouth. "Sounds good to me," I said. Amanda and I jumped up and headed for the common house.

When we got there, just about everybody staying at the Cottages was already seated. I saw Annette and Carl Moscowitz, each holding a baby, sitting next to Tessa and her parents. Jeremy Wilson was roaming around with a half-eaten ice-cream sandwich in his hand, looking for a seat. The Buxtons were sitting near my family, probably because Max insisted on being with Viola and Helena. Juliet and Sally were hanging out near the back of the room, while Derek sat with his parents near the door. Jack and Rita Carson were up front with Duchess and Patrick and Sam, and Rinker was pulling more folding chairs off a cart and opening them up so everyone could have a seat.

Cap'n Teddy stood on the little raised platform at one end of the room and cleared his throat. He was wearing his yachting cap again. He held out his arms. "Welcome, everybody. Hope you enjoyed your dinner!"

We all burst into applause. "*Olé!*" I heard Poppy call.

"Did everybody get an ice-cream sandwich?" he asked. "If not, come on up and get one. Don't be shy." He gestured toward the freezer. Then he cleared his throat again. "This isn't easy to say," he began, looking a lot more serious than the Cap'n Teddy I was used to.

"As some of you may have guessed, Paradise Cottages is in financial trouble." He stopped and cleared his throat. "For a while there, we even thought we might have to give up the place, sell out to a developer."

I glanced at Mike Buxton. He was listening to every word.

"But I'm pleased to report tonight that we'll be in business for the rest of this summer, and for next summer, and — hopefully — for every summer after that!" Cap'n Teddy nodded and smiled. "Duchess and I have always felt that everyone who comes here is family. Now we know that's true. Dave Parker, could you come up here?"

Poppy! What did he have to do with this?

Poppy worked his way to the front of the room, and Cap'n Teddy threw an arm around him. "David and his family have been coming to the Cottages for — how long, Dave?"

Poppy beamed. "Twelve wonderful years," he reported.

I looked over at Mom and saw her smiling up at Poppy. She seemed to know what was going on. In fact, a lot of people in the room were smiling. What was up?

Cap'n Teddy explained it all. "This morning,"

he said, "Dave and a couple of others came to see me. They'd come up with a plan — a plan to save Paradise." He gave Poppy a little shove forward. "Tell them about it, Dave," he said.

Poppy looked a little sheepish. He ducked his head. "It's nothing fancy," he said. "Just that we all agreed that we'd like to help out, be even more a part of this place. From now on, all the regular tenants of Paradise will be part owners, too. Just a tiny part — the Drysdales will still be the main owners. But the rest of us will have a stake, too. And that means we'll be helping out. Rebuilding buildings that have" — he faltered a little, obviously not wanting to mention the fires just then — "been destroyed. Painting a little here, doing a little landscaping there. Just routine maintenance, really. To keep Paradise alive. To keep it the heavenly place that we all know and love." He stepped back a little, and people started to clap. Then he stepped up again and held up his hands. "I just want to acknowledge Mike Buxton as one of the folks who came up with this plan. He came to me this morning and said he was ready with his checkbook and hammer. Said he'd been saying so to his wife all along, since they've come to love this place as much as the rest of us do. So, thanks, Mike! We'll depend on your expertise as we go along!"

He stepped back again, and everybody started

clapping and whistling and yelling. I glanced over at Helena and Viola. They were grinning back at me. So much for Mike Buxton plotting to take over the Cottages!

The fact was, we were *all* going to take over the place. With any luck, I'll be bringing *my* kids here someday. I can't wait to show them all the things I love. I can't wait to welcome them to Paradise.

About the Author

Ellen Miles lives in a small house in Vermont with her large dog, Django, who can eat a maple creemee in the time it takes to say "maple creemee." She has one brother and one sister, both older, and while she loves her siblings, she always thought it might be fun to have many more of them. One of her all-time favorite books is *Harriet the Spy*. She loves to ride her bike in the summer and ski in the winter, so Vermont is the perfect place for her to live.